May 24, 1607

We are back at the for̶[...] assigned to strip tree bark and to keep [...] the ground to secure the walls.

But my heart is sick. It is all I can do to keep my mind from the terror I saw in Richard's eyes when we left him behind with those savages. What is happening to him now? What is his fate? And the last words between us were angry. It is too late to take them back, but they haunt me.

Nicholas Skot and Samuel Collier have become skittish. They work at dragging wood from forest to fort, but like Richard, neither is a large boy. I told them what happened to Richard, and they wonder if they will be the next to be traded if there is a need. Back on the ship I would have enjoyed the fear I see in Samuel's eyes, but now it is only a reminder of Richard's fate. Nicholas has told me he will run to the woods before being taken like a sheep to slaughter at the hands of John Smith.

Smith. I know the captain is brave and strong and does what he deems right, but I know now that I do not want to be a man like Smith.

And so when my mind has a moment of rest from thoughts of Richard I wonder—who should I imitate? Where is a man I can act like? Where is a man I can become?

Tor Books by Elizabeth Massie

Young Founders #1: 1870: Not with our Blood
Young Founders #2: 1609: Winter of the Dead

YOUNG FOUNDERS'

1609:

WINTER OF THE DEAD

A Novel about the Founding of Jamestown

Elizabeth Massie

TOR®

A TOM DOHERTY ASSOCIATES BOOK
NEW YORK

This is a work of fiction. All the characters and events portrayed in this book are either products of the author's imagination or are used fictitiously.

YOUNG FOUNDERS #2: 1609: WINTER OF THE DEAD

Copyright © 2000 by Elizabeth Massie

A Tor Book
Published by Tom Doherty Associates, LLC
175 Fifth Avenue
New York, NY 10010

www.tor.com

Tor® is a registered trademark of Tom Doherty Associates, LLC.

ISBN: 0-812-59093-7

First edition: March 2000

Printed in the United States of America

0 9 8 7 6 5 4 3 2 1

To my mother, Patricia Spilman, outstanding artist, mother, and a very wise woman. You encouraged in me a freedom of spirit, a peace of self, tolerance, compassion, and the wings to fly forward to new places. I love you!

❧ Introduction ❧

THERE WAS A story told among the Powhatans in the late sixteenth century that strangers from across the great waters would come and destroy their people. The strange men would have golden hair, be of light skin, and would carry sticks that spit fire. That story came true.

In 1607 three ships arrived on the shores of what is now the state of Virginia, carrying adventurers from across the Atlantic Ocean. These voyagers did indeed have fair skin and hair, and they brought with them tools, swords, and strange heavy objects that shot fire from their muzzles—muskets and pistols.

With great hardship, disappointment, and determination, these men established the first permanent English settlement in the New World. Gentlemen, sailors, and laborers made the difficult voyage for the purpose of finding gold and riches for the Virginia Company of London, an organization of wealthy men who financed the expedition and who expected a good return on their investments. And among the men who made the trip, there were also teenaged boys, young

men with as much desire for adventure as those older
than they.

"Hostage exchange" was common practice with
many explorers in the sixteenth and seventeenth cen-
turies. It was seen as prudent by seasoned adventurers
to have boys in their early to mid teens to be used as
commodities to trade—like beads, tools, or other trinkets—to the natives of strange, new lands. Sometimes
these boys were considered permanent "goodwill gifts";
other times they were traded for a native as a "cultural
exchange"; other times a boy was expected to live
among the natives, learn the language and customs,
then escape and return to the explorers in order to
convey all they had learned, thus giving the explorers
an advantage. Whether these boys knew why they had
been brought on a particular voyage is unclear; they
may have believed they had been selected to be chop-
pers of wood, builders of homes and fortress walls,
bearers of arms, and haulers of water. For if they had
truly known their destiny, would they have agreed to
the long sea journey in the first place?

It is recorded that two boys—Thomas Savage in 1608
and Henry Spilman in 1609—were among the ex-
changes made between the Powhatans and the men of
the Jamestown settlement. These two boys lived to
adulthood, served as interpreters during the later years
in Jamestown, and wrote about their experiences.

But what of the other boys who came to America
with John Smith and Christopher Newport? Their experiences were certainly as traumatic and exciting as
those of the others who sailed on the *Susan Constant*,
the *Godspeed*, and the *Discovery*. Nathaniel Peacock and
Richard Mutton were real people, two of the young
men on the original journey in 1607. What happened
to them? Did they live? Did they die during the cruel
summers and winters of the early years, when the set-

tlement was on the verge of collapse, when natives were attacking with a vengeance and disease was rampant and starvation became so intense that some men took to robbing the graves of the dead to find meat?

Here is a story of what these boys might have faced, set against the backdrop of true and often horrific events. Many of these characters were real people. Nathaniel and Richard were small players in a dramatic portion of United States history. Yet to these boys, the part they played was frightening, challenging, and personal.

1

March 11, 1607

At last, praise God, the Susan Constant has eased its rolling and I am able to write. For 50 days we have been sailing from London across these wretched waters, and for these many days we have been biding our time, some not as well as others. Unlike some men down here on the 'tween deck, I have a strong stomach and the pitching of the ship rarely bothers me. But the other passengers, many gentlemen and wealthy fortune-seekers, whine like babies when we rock back and forth in the waves. They complain and then they vomit. It isn't the jarring sea which makes me sick, but those prissy men and the fact that I am responsible for cleaning up what they spit out. Yet I must act like they do not bother me. They do not like me, but it is best that I act humble and stupid so they will leave me alone.

Gentlemen. I've never had to spend so much time in so close quarters. Back in London, I could run from them and put distance between us, but not here. Here, I must endure them. Here, each one of us is trying to make a "home" out of a space of perhaps two feet wide and five feet long. Some of the gentlemen who boarded first laid claim to barrels, maneuvered them so they were side by side, and put their mattresses across the tops so they would not have to sleep on the floor. Others have nailed canvas sheets from the ceiling in order to make themselves little private closets. As a simple laborer, and a boy at that, I was required to find my space last. I sleep here, near the stern, under the clacking tiller which thumps constantly as it works the rudder. The other commoners here on the Susan Constant mind their own business and fraternize primarily with each other. They do not bother me, but they have not befriended me, either.

My name is Nathaniel Peacock. I am fifteen years of age, born on the 15th of February in the year of our Lord 1592. It has been a very long time since I've held a pen to write. Paper and ink are hard to come by for such as myself, a poor orphan boy from the London streets. But I won't be a poor boy for long. Soon I will be a rich man with all the money and goods I want, because we are going to Virginia, a land of beauty and wealth, named for the Virgin Queen Elizabeth who reigned until 1603, the time when our King James ascended the throne. In this land of Virginia I shall be able to act as I want and not as I must.

My written words are awkward and splotched, as much from unfamiliarity with this pen as from the shifting of the ship on the water. But as long as I can get my hands on ink and paper, I intend to keep a journal of my adventures.

We have been traveling since December 20th of last year. It's been a much longer journey than planned. We have faced sleet and rain and thunderous waves. Twice we've gone six-on-four rations as commanded by Captain Newport, allowing six men the food of four so we do not run out before we find an island on which to refresh our supplies. We have seen the near-death of our Reverend Hunt from seasickness and have seen his miraculous recovery. But we are together still, and still are headed west.

There are three ships crossing the ocean—the Susan Constant, the Discovery, and the Godspeed. The London Company, a group of rich men seeking yet more fortune, raised the *money for the ships and the crew and the supplies to take this voyage. The Company named Bartholomew Gosnold to be captain of the* Godspeed, *and they named John Ratcliffe to be captain of the* Discovery. *Here on the* Susan Constant *the solemn Captain Christopher Newport is in charge. It did surprise Richard and me that John Smith wasn't named captain of this ship. Smith, as everyone knows, is a brave and daring man indeed.*

It was John Smith himself who spotted my companion, Richard Mutton, and me outside the Charging Boar Tavern in London last September, and offered us the chance to sail the sea to Virginia. We had been stealing from the passersby as was our usual morning activity, and at first when Smith called to me, I was certain he had seen me take a coin pouch from an old man. To be caught stealing small things in London is to be beaten. To be caught stealing valuables is to be hanged, and I daresay what I'd taken from the old codger had value. But Smith hadn't witnessed the theft. He merely bowed to us and then asked if we were healthy and free to travel. I hesitated, but when he introduced himself as Smith, I assured him right away that we were indeed of good health and free to go wherever he wanted us to go.

Smith said there was a voyage to go to the New World of Virginia in December. I said yes. I also said I could use hammer and nails and an axe, that I could tend animals, could cook, and could fight with musket or sword. All lies, of course, but to get by in this world, one must act many roles. Richard was not as enthusiastic as I to go. He was afraid the gentlemen on the trip would treat us poorly. Why, Richard reasoned, should we get on a ship to be treated poorly in close quarters when we could be treated just as poorly in London where we had room to run away? But I say you must act whatever part you are given at whatever moment that is, and soon you will get what you want. If we act as humble laborers, then we will survive the voyage to gain the wealth we so deserve in Virginia. We could never get wealthy in London, no matter how many old men we robbed. But the Spanish have found gold on their voyages west and so shall we. In Virginia, I've heard tell there is gold lying about the ground, just waiting to be picked up and put into one's pocket.

The blotch on the paper just now is where my hand jerked, throwing off a rat who had nuzzled up to my elbow and proposed to be my friend. I think he's wandered off to bed down with one of the gentlemen.

Poor rat.

I stole this paper, the pen, and the inkwell from the wooden box of Samuel Collier, John Smith's brattish page. The boy is red-haired and freckle-faced and believes he is better than me although he is two years my junior. He has a mattress near Richard's and mine, on the other side of a pea barrel and potato barrel. I know how to play the part of meek laborer in front of the men, but Samuel best watch it if he finds himself alone with me.

In spite of the others' complaints, my companion Richard Mutton and I are bearing the trip well. We do what we're told, running errands, bringing food to the men, cleaning rubbish and wastes, killing rats and mice and tossing them overboard, mending loose boards alongside the sailors. Sometimes we make a game of throwing the rats, to see who can pitch one the farthest. I usually win. Whatever our tasks and however poorly the men on the Susan Constant treat us, I keep thinking of the reasons Richard and I came along in the first place.

There are, of course, the reasons the London Company gives for our venture. Those are of bringing profits to the Company and of establishing a settlement in Virginia where English goods can be shipped in exchange for New World commodities.

There are the reasons King James gives, those of spreading Christianity to the heathens of Virginia, finding a route to the East India Sea, and establishing a stronghold in Virginia to halt the further spread of Spain and France's claims between the 34th and 45th degrees of north latitude.

But Richard's and my hearts are set on our own expectations. And dreams of them make everything worthwhile.
Riches. Treasure.
Gold!

2

THERE WAS MOVEMENT across the 'tween deck, a sound of shoes clattering on wood. Nathaniel Peacock glanced up, brushed a strand of matted brown hair from his eyes, and squinted. It was late at night, well after suppertime. In the faint lights of the lanterns scattered around where the gentlemen and other workers lounged, Nathaniel could see red-haired Samuel Collier climbing down the ladder from the main deck. The boy was wearing his hat, the broad-brimmed black one with the jaunty, bouncing feather.

Quickly Nat capped the inkwell and slipped it and the pen beneath his mattress. Then he lay down, keeping his eyes open to slits to watch the approach of the page. In one hand he held the papers of his journal close by his side, hoping they would dry soon so he could stash them safely under his straw-stuffed pallet. In his other hand he held the five pebbles he'd scooped up from the River Thames shore, a last connection to the world he'd left behind. Beside Nathaniel, fourteen-year-old Richard Mutton slept on his own lumpy mattress.

Samuel worked his way carefully through the clusters

of gentlemen and commoners on the floor. As were Nathaniel and Richard, Samuel was always cautious not to disturb the men. Even though tonight most were preoccupied—playing cards, rolling dice, chewing the remainders of their evening meal of hardtack and cold pork, coaxing tunes from flutes, sipping beer from mugs, and fumbling with lanterns in an attempt to make them burn more brightly—one misstep from a boy could send any of them into a rage. An upset gentleman was a dreadful experience. Nathaniel, for doing nothing more than spilling gruel or sloshing waste water, had been punched in the ear and kicked in the gut.

When Samuel found his mattress, he paused and put his hands on his hips and frowned as if something was wrong. Could the boy tell that Nathaniel had been into his wooden storage box?

Samuel drew his nose up and sniffed the air. This close, even in the pale light of the lanterns across the floor, Nathaniel could see his twitchy blue eyes and his bright red hair.

"Something stinks," Samuel said.

Nathaniel said nothing. Samuel was constantly trying to pick a fight, and if Nathaniel was going to match wits with this boy, he'd do it on his own terms and in his own place, not here with witnesses. Instead, he closed his eyes and pretended to doze.

"You hear me, Peacock? I said something stinks, and I think it's you, you London vermin! What was Smith thinking to invite you and Mutton along? Such a waste of space, I say. Illiterates and indigents! Pah! We have been so much better to have brought along a few extra pigs. At least pigs are worth their weight in victuals!" He waited as if he hoped Nathaniel would jump up and get himself in trouble. Even though Samuel was of less status than any of the men, Nathaniel and Richard were less than Samuel, and an outright fight within earshot of the gentlemen would likely bring about more of a punishment for Nat than for Samuel.

Nathaniel said nothing.

"Waste of space." This time Samuel's words were softer, as if he was speaking to himself. Clearly he thought Nathaniel was sleeping.

A moment later, Nat heard the page shuffle around beneath his thin blanket and then go still.

Go to sleep, you spoiled puppy, Nat thought.

Then, when the ink was dry on the page, he hid the paper behind the barrel at his head. He lay flat, crossed his arms beneath his head, and stared up at the low 'tween deck ceiling. The five pebbles were cool in his fist.

The boat hull creaked. The cannons, poised at shuttered portholes, bumped back and forth on their blocks. From the hold below the 'tween deck, Nat could hear the sheep and pigs and chickens in their crates bleating and grunting and squawking to each other. The ship's tiller just above and behind Nat's head thumped steadily as it worked the rudder, taking them farther across the sea toward Virginia. The bell rang from the upper deck, indicating it was time for a change of watch.

Nathaniel watched the light from the men's lanterns cast eerie, dancing shadows about the barrels and hull. Some of the shadows were shapeless and vague; others reminded him of things he'd left behind in London. One moved like the jaws of a mad dog which had bitten through the leg of his trousers the day the ships had left the port at Blackwall. Richard had seen it as a bad omen for the trip, but Nat had seen it as a good omen because the dog had missed the flesh of Nat's leg entirely. One shadow fluttered like a swan on the Thames River, and another hovered like a stray cloud in London's oft gray sky.

Unlike Richard, Nathaniel did not miss the reeking old English city. Nat had been born there, and had been raised by his mother, a barmaid, until he was six and she had died of fever. Cast out by the bar's owner, Nat had lived on the streets and had slept in various stables and barns until, nearly a year later, he was taken in by a street peddler who sold fish from a rattly push-cart. Nat had helped the man catch and hawk his goods, and the man had given Nat food and shelter in the man's shack. He'd also given Nat something most street boys would never have. He'd taught Nat to read and write.

The peddler, a large and cheerful man called Boonie, had been as poor as any beggar, but the man had a love for literature, and had kept a tattered but beloved collection of books in a little chest. From these, Nat had learned to read, and on paper scrounged by Boonie Nat had learned to write. It seemed as if only the rich had paper, ink, and quills, but somehow Boonie would bring these things home and the two of them would write. Nat was certain the man had stolen the paper and ink, but it didn't matter. He had a skill that the gentlemen had, and it would serve him someday. But he had never told anyone, not even Richard. Some secrets were best kept close.

Nat was nine when Boonie had died from a mule kick to the head, and Nat had lived alone ever since. He had formed partnerships with other street boys, taking what food and clothing and bits of coal they could in order to survive. But the partnerships had come and gone. Some of the boys had been caught at their thievery; others had stolen from Nathaniel and run away. Some of the boys had died. Not long after Nat's eleventh birthday, he'd met Richard. The two worked as a team in snatching vegetables from street-side stands or lifting valuables from rich women's baskets, but Nat didn't consider Richard a friend.

Nat rolled over onto his elbows and took the ink and pen back from under his mattress. Laying the pebbles aside, he smoothed the paper as best he could on the tiny floor space by his mattress, squinted in the murky light, and wrote,

It is a good thing not to have friends. They can betray you. They can die. A man alone has the most power. A man alone shares with no one, and is the better for it. A man alone is truly a man.

And at last, with the rhythmic rocking of the ship, Nathaniel let sleep take him away for a little while.

❧ 3 ❧

March 13, 1607

Nat and Richard stood on the main deck in the bright sun and cool breeze, hurling rats and mice over the rail into the ocean waves. There had been seven buckets full of the vermin, some caught among the barrels and the gentlemen's pallets on the 'tween deck, others on the main deck and in the cook's small brick galley. One particularly large and hairy rat had bedded down with the overweight and haughty man Edward Brookes, and the man had shrieked like a woman until Nat had clubbed the rodent with a poker.

As of yet, Richard and Nat hadn't had to go down through the square hatch in the floor of the 'tween deck into the lightless hold and catch rats down there. So far, only the sailors had swung down on their ropes to feed the animals and to work the pumps. The 'tween deck was smelly indeed, with the sweat and expensive perfumes worn by the gentlemen, but the fumes that drifted up from the hold were far worse. Who knew what kinds of creatures made their home down there among the waters of the bilge? And Nathaniel knew

that Richard was claustrophobic, especially in unfamil-
iar, unlit places. It had taken the boy a few weeks to
lose his discomfort on the 'tween deck.

Catching and dumping rats was preferable to other
chores the two boys were given. It was much more fun
to collect the animals and play at who could toss one
farther than it was to clean spilled urine or to swab
down vomit.

"Look!" Nat said to Richard, nudging him on the
arm as the rat he'd tossed arched and dropped into
the water a good thirty feet from the ship. "Aha! Quite
a distance old ratty flew there! I'm winning."

"My last one was at least that far," grumbled Richard.
"We can't be certain, can we? Who shall go out to mea-
sure?"

"Your arms are just too short," said Nat, grinning.

Richard scooped another rat from his bucket and
threw it, but a gust of wind kept it from going very far.
The little dead creature, its toes curled and its glazed
eyes open, dropped only ten feet from the ship.

"Pah!" grumped Richard.

But Richard's less-than-cheerful humor didn't
bother Nathaniel. The day was too pleasant, the sun
too kind, to make him think of anything but what lay
ahead. In not many weeks, they would step off onto the
land of Virginia, where gold and pearls abounded,
where urchin boys could become gentlemen and pompous pages would give them the respect they deserved.

"It seems to me that Samuel Collier would better
serve this trip killing rats and mice than to do whatever
silly errands John Smith has him do," said Richard. He
ran his hand under his nose, wiping away sooty mucus
from a lingering case of sniffles. "I hate the page."

"So do I," said Nat. "But as I've told you, you must
act as if he does not offend you. Stay out of his way.

Act as if he does not exist and we will be the better for it."

"I cannot ignore him. He constantly chides us!"

"But we must act our station so the men will leave us alone as much as possible. When we get to Virginia, we can improve our status. We can even steal silver and pearls and run away to live in a gold-filled Virginia hill if we want! But until then, we must be quiet, dim-witted laborers."

"I hate the gentlemen, too," said Richard. "They see us as no more than stray cats on a London alley."

"Behave as a cat and you will be seen as a cat. Behave like a humble ship's boy and you will be seen thus."

Richard rolled his eyes and gestured with upturned hands. "I cannot act as well as you! You have always been able to make people believe what you want them to. You could play a part at the Globe Theatre, I am certain. But not me, I—"

"Stop chattering!" It was a sailor who had seen the boys pause in their work. "I'll clout you! Back to work!"

"Yes, sir!" said Nat. Richard scowled.

"Only one more rat for us each," said Nathaniel, looking into the buckets. "Here is your chance to best me."

Nat and Richard threw their rats at the same time. Nat's went much farther than Richard's, plopping into the foamy green water and then disappearing.

"Idiot's game," said Richard.

"Ah, but it gives us the chance to stay above deck a bit longer, Richard," said Nat. "If we dumped them all at once, we'd have to go back down at once, and I don't know about you, but I prefer fresh air to stale."

"Hmm," said Richard.

The boys stood for a few more seconds, staring out at the vast water, pretending to toss rats from the now empty buckets. All around them, sailors went about their business, checking riggings, climbing the fore-mast, the mizzenmast, and the mainmast to constantly check and alter the sails, shouting to each other and to the crews of the *Discovery* and the *Godspeed* not far away. The huge white sails on the three ships billowed, and the red and white St. George's Cross flags snapped briskly in the wind. Over the past few days, there had been rough weather and the cook had been forced to put out the fire in his oven so a stray spark would not set the ship afire. Today, however, Nat could smell sweet, roasting meat from the small galley under the Great Cabin.

Nathaniel and Richard were in the clothes they'd worn since they had left London. Both had moth-ruined wool breeches, ratty silk stockings, weather-hardened leather shoes, and simple white linen blouses. Nathaniel also owned a brown cloak, given him by the charitable wife of a wheelwright who lived in Downing Street near the Thames. The cloak was now part of his mattress, covering the straw-filled bag to keep it less scratchy.

"How are you faring, my men?" came a familiar voice. John Smith stood with his arms crossed by the mainmast. Even though he was dressed as dandy as any lord, with a velvet doublet and cloak, embroidered breeches, silk stockings, and pistol and dagger at his waist, it was clear he had felt the effects of the long journey; his face was drawn and more pale and his cheekbones were prominent. Yet his voice was strong and his head held high. Smith often had a kind word for those below his station, and it was a pleasant dis-traction for Nat and Richard.

"Fine, sir," said Nat, bowing obediently. "It looks as though we'll have good weather for a time. Praise God."

"Praise God indeed," said Smith. He strode to the

railing and with a smile said, "Watch." He held out an open hand, showed it to Nat and Richard, then closed it and gave it a shake. When he opened it again, there was a shilling where none had been.

Nat's eyes widened. "How did you make that appear?"

"Oh," said Smith. "I have learned a lot in my travels. I have learned how to make things appear and disappear. This can be very useful at times. Very useful indeed."

"I can imagine," said Nat. So, not only was Smith dramatic and loud and confident, he was good at sleight of hand. What an amazing life this man must lead. *I would like to be just like him someday*, Nat thought.

But as Smith moved the shilling from one hand to the other, his face grew somber. He glanced over his shoulder. Captain Newport and Captain Gabriel Archer had come out of the Great Cabin beneath the stern's quarterdeck and stood talking quietly and looking at Smith. Newport was tall with broad shoulders and very little hair. Archer had a narrow face and fidgety eyes.

"The bad weather may have calmed," Smith said softly, "but the environment on this ship is more unpredictable now than ever. It will not be long before we are embroiled in a great turmoil."

Richard frowned. Nat said, "What . . . ?" But then he knew it was best to keep quiet. Best to act like he didn't understand. But he did understand. Many of the gentlemen on the ship didn't like Smith. They were jealous of him and thought he was too arrogant. Often they grumbled about his attitude. Now it seemed as if the other captains might also feel the same way. This couldn't be good for the voyage. With some luck or perhaps some divine interference, the men would keep their distrust to themselves and not cause any trouble before they reached the shores of Virginia. Not only was there the peril of rough seas, unpredictable winds on a long trip such as this, there were also Spanish ships on this very same sea who would welcome the chance to attack and rob an English ship. If the men fought seriously among themselves, they would be less able to deal with other dangers they might meet.

But then Smith smiled and clapped Nat and Richard on the shoulders. "And where is my page, that good-for-nothing? Go send him to me. I have errands which need to be done. If he's sleeping, douse him with water!" With a chuckle, Smith walked away, past Archer and Newport, who paused to watch him and then began talking again.

Down below, men were talking, coughing, and spitting. As always, Nat had to pause on the ladder to regain his vision in the dim light. Then he and Richard placed the buckets behind the base of the ladder and wormed through the men to their pallets. Nearby, on his own rumpled mattress, Samuel sat glaring at the two boys. He held his open wooden box in his lap.

"Samuel," Nat said. "Smith is calling for you."

"Yes," said Richard. "He is furious. I've never seen his face so red or his hands so palsied!"

"You," hissed Samuel, without making a move to get up.

"You?" said Nat. "You what?"

"You urchins," Samuel said.

"I beg your pardon for being an urchin," said Nat. "But such is my fate. Forgive me for my worthlessness."

Samuel's eyes drew up and his lip quivered furiously. "You've stolen from me, you stinking beggars!"

"I don't know what you mean," said Nat. Richard dropped to his mattress, already bored with this game of words.

Samuel shook his head. "I'm missing paper and ink,

and no one but you would have the nature to steal."

"Paper?" said Nat. "Why do you think I'd steal paper? Certainly I can't read nor write, I haven't your education."

"You are sneaky and clever!" Samuel snipped. "Just wait, you won't know when my revenge is coming! You two just wait and see!" He slammed his black hat onto his head and stormed away, the feather bouncing.

"What do you think he will try?" asked Richard. "I have never heard him so angry."

"Who knows and who can care?" said Nat.

"Did you steal his paper and ink?"

"Why would I? I am as ignorant of letters as you. Now come. We have work to do."

The day went on as usual, emptying waste, serving food, washing out the most severely soiled clothing of the gentlemen with seawater, repairing loose planks alongside the sailors.

But that night, after all had turned in for the evening's rest, Richard's yell woke Nat with a start.

Sitting bolt upright and blinking the cloud of sleep away, Nat looked to his right where Richard slept. Richard was not there. He then heard Samuel's voice, near the center of the 'tween deck. "Catch them, urchin! You will need them in Virginia!"

"Give them to me!"

Nat jumped up, hopping over sleeping men, trying not to step on anyone's head.

"Samuel!" shouted Richard.

Men were awakening now, yelling and complaining.

"You boys shut your mouths or I'll shut them for you!"

"What is the commotion?"

"I'll give you a wallop if you do not quiet down!"

Nat found his way to the center of the 'tween deck, his eyes now adjusted enough to see what was going on. Samuel had pried the wooden grating from the hold's hatch, and was dangling Richard's shoes over the hole. Richard was reaching out for them, but clearly afraid that if he made a quick move, Samuel would indeed drop the shoes down into the stinking black pit at the bottom of the ship.

"Samuel, give me the bloody shoes!" Richard said.

"Give me my paper and ink back."

"I don't have your paper. Give me my shoes."

"Be quiet, boys!" shouted Edward Brookes. "You will go over the side of this ship into the ocean if I get my wish!"

Nat said, "Samuel, give Richard his shoes before the men beat us!"

"No!" Samuel giggled and threw the shoes into the hold.

Richard gasped, then grabbed Samuel by the collar. "You worthless beast! I need my shoes!"

"Then go get them. I will not stop you. If you need your shoes, by all means, go into the hold and get them."

Suddenly there was a whoosh and a blow, and Nat was struck to his side, his breath knocked out. He lay stunned, struggling to pull air back into his lungs. Edward Brookes then knocked Samuel over, but Richard jumped out of the way in time.

"You boys get to your places before I kill the whole of you!" Brookes said. "And I am a man of my word!"

Samuel groaned, sat up, and said, "I will go, sir. Do not strike me again."

Brookes grunted once more, then, seeming somewhat satisfied, stumbled back to his mattress.

Samuel said quietly to Richard, "Best be after your shoes, boy. I would not be in Virginia with my feet bare. It could be dangerous and quite cold." Then he giggled and walked away.

"My shoes," Richard said, almost as if in mourning.

"I will help you get them in the morning when it is light," said Nat.

"My shoes are leather, and there are more vermin down there than anywhere else on this ship," said Richard. His voice was shaky. "If I wait until tomorrow, they will be chewed to scraps. I will go down now. I have no choice."

"We do not have a lantern, Richard. If I try to borrow one from a gentleman, he will say I am stealing, you know it. Stealing will have me whipped and then tossed overboard."

"All I need is rope. I think the shoes went straight down, so if I go straight down, too, I should find them without too much trouble."

Nat nodded reluctantly. He went to the ladder and found a length of rope coiled on a nail on its side. He tied one end around the bottom rung of the ladder, then took the length to Richard. All around, men flopped over on their mattresses in various stages of sleep, snoring, burping, farting. Richard grasped the rope, whispered, "God help me, I never wanted to go down into that dreadful place," and lowered himself into the hold.

Nat could imagine what was down there with Richard—water snakes swimming in standing water, enormous rats grown fat and vicious with constant feeding on the men's food supplies and an occasional caged chicken. He shivered and gooseflesh stood up on his arms and neck.

"I've never smelled such foul odors," Richard called up.

"Shh! Get the shoes quickly. I'll pull you back up."

There was silence for a few moments, then the sound of Richard swearing as he rummaged below, feeling for the shoes. All around Nat, the men began snoring once more.

Hurry! Get out of that wretched place!

Nat leaned over a bit farther, straining to hear, hoping Richard would not be bit by something poisonous.

And then there was a shrill giggle immediately behind Nat and something struck him between his shoulder blades and he was tumbling headlong into the rancid darkness of the hold. He landed on his side with an "umph!" His left arm was twisted beneath him, and hot, stabbing pains shot through it.

A voice very near him said, "Nat! Is that you?"

Nat croaked, "Samuel knocked me down into this place!"

"The cursed brat!"

Nat got his feet beneath him and stood dizzily. The flooring was as he feared, slimy and damp and uneven. The smell down here was worse than he could have imagined. It was like sticking his head into a waste bucket full of excrement.

"Are you all right? Did you break anything?"

Nat moved his left arm and gritted his teeth against sparkles of pain that traveled the length of it. "I think not. My arm can move, but it hurts dreadfully. God! I cannot have a broken arm. How would I survive the rest of the journey with a broken arm?"

"You can move it truly?" asked Richard.

"Yes."

"Then it is not broken. Perhaps bruised or sprained."

"Yes," said Nat. Then he heard a hissing sound, and the chickens nearby squawked.

"Snakes, Nathaniel!" cried Richard.

"No, I don't think so."

"Or huge, rabid rats like the dog back in London. We cannot see them before they bite us on the legs!"

"Richard, the hissing sound is only water running in

the bilge. Be calm or you will only make matters worse."

"How can they be worse?"

There was a pause, and Nat said, "At this moment, I do not really know." Then, "Did you find your shoes?"

"I found one of them."

"We have to find the other, then we must get out of here straightaway."

Then Richard said, "How?"

"How? What do you mean?"

"You have a hurt arm. How will you get out of here?"

"I . . . ," Nat began. But Richard was right. Richard could pull himself up the rope, but there was no way Nat could do it with only one good arm. "I do not know."

"Don't fret," Richard said, the fear in his voice barely disguised. "We'll find a way. But first the shoe."

Nat swallowed and his throat was dry.

It took a while to find the shoe. Nat grimaced as he felt around the filthy flooring, around crates and barrels as he held his bad arm close to his body. He tried not to think of things waiting in the darkness to bite his fingertips, but every strange sound and sensation caused him to draw his hands back in terror.

And then Richard said, "I have it!"

Nat stood up. His knees were soaked through with stinking water, and his hands were scratched and full of splinters. His arm throbbed.

"Get the rope now and climb out," said Nat.

"What about you?"

"Go on without me. Maybe my arm will heal enough in a day or two and then you can throw the rope back down to me. If not, I'll just stay down here until we land, and if I am not dead, they can take me out with the chickens and pigs."

There was silence, then Richard broke into laughter.

"You are such an actor, Nat! What drama! Now hear me. When I am out, I'll toss the rope back to you. You tie it about your waist and I will haul you up."

"You're not strong enough."

"This trip is making a man of me. Just wait and see."

There was a deep breath and grunt, and Richard was climbing the rope. Nat could feel the air move as Richard's legs kicked out, working to hoist his body upward. A minute later, the whispered call came from above. "Catch the rope now and tie it tightly!"

Nat's hand felt around until it found the rope. He pulled at it to get enough length to put it around himself.

But it was too short.

He pulled again and met with taut resistance. "Richard, the rope is too short to make a loop!"

A quiet curse from above, then Richard said, "Let me find more rope and we will tie them together."

Nat stood in the stinking darkness, not wanting to move now that he was alone in the hold. Visions of tremendous rats sprang into his mind again, and he wished he had tall leather boots like a captain to protect his ankles.

Then Richard's voice came. "Nat, there is no more rope to be found here on the 'tween deck."

"What do you propose, then? That I stay here and rot?"

"Quit whining. I will find more rope in the day, when it is light and I am allowed up deck. Find a barrel. I will have rope in just a few hours. Be patient."

Nat stretched his hand out and moved forward until he found a barrel. He sat atop it and stared out into nothingness.

"Goodnight, Nat," called Richard.

"It is not very good, but what can I do about it?"

Richard swore softly, then was gone.

Nat drew his legs up and crossed them. *There are no poisonous snakes nor rats with deadly jaws,* he told himself. But he kept his legs crossed and away from the floor just in case. His mind went fuzzy, and even though he fought to stay awake, he fell into a restless sleep.

Rope smacking against his cheek made him startle into consciousness. His eyes flew open.

"What?" he said. "Where am I?" Then he remembered. But it wasn't day. Who had lowered rope into the hold while it was still nighttime? He squinted up into the darkness, but could see nothing but the outline of a head.

"Quick," said a man's voice. "Loop this around yourself and tie it tightly. I will get you up."

Nat reached for the rope. His left arm was still sore and now it felt swollen. Carefully he drew the end around himself and tied it, then slid the loop up beneath his arms and took hold. He stood up on the barrel. It was only a matter of six or so feet to the hatch.

"All right, Nat," said the mysterious man. "Pull."

The rope went rigid and lifted Nat up off the barrel a few inches. But then he slammed back down again.

Nat said, "I lost my grip. I am too heavy!"

"Shhh, do not make a business of this," said the man. "The gentlemen are still asleep and I would like to keep it that way. Let me get you out quickly. Hold tight."

The rope inched up. Nat tried to will himself to weigh less by loosening his body's joints. The rope went up another four inches. Then it wavered, but didn't slip. It was pulled jerkily yet consistently upward, and in just a few moments, Nat was able to throw one foot up through the hatch, then another, and then he was pulled to the safety of the 'tween deck floor.

"How is your arm?" asked the man.

"It will be better soon," answered Nat. He pulled

himself out of the rope and then squinted at the man who had helped him. It was Jehu Robinson, a thin, very quiet man whose pallet was near the ladder.

"Thank you," Nat said uncomfortably.

Jehu looked over at the mattresses, occupied by dozing gentlemen, then back at Nat. "I am ashamed these men would not help you," he said. "We could all hear you. They are not all asleep, but hiding with their eyes closed. I suspect they are afraid to dirty their hands or bring out a callus on those smooth, unblemished palms."

Nat said nothing. He didn't know what role to play with this unusual man.

"God forgive us our selfishness," said Jehu. "Now, let us get back to our places before the gentlemen decide our yammering is so bothersome that we should both be dumped down into that hold!"

4

March 20, 1607

OVER THE DAYS that followed, there was nothing to see in the ocean but waves, an occasional fish leaping into the air, the fins of sharks slicing the water, and the other ships, sails stretched full, following behind. *Virginia*, thought Nat. *Where are you?* But the minutes on the upper deck were the best entertainment to be had, and Nat relished them. They took their time dumping urine and rodents into the water so they could savor the fresh air. At least Nat's arm was not broken and only ached on occasion.

One cloudy afternoon, as Nat and Richard stared out at the sparkling waves, tossing rats, an argument brewed behind them.

Nat recognized Gabriel Archer's voice immediately. He didn't think it would be wise to acknowledge the disagreement, so he looked ahead at the water, while tuning his ears in sharply. He held his finger to his lips so Richard would follow suit.

"Sir, I have often told you that Captain Smith is a troublemaker. His haughty attitude with the gentlemen has made him so loathsome I scarce can tolerate it. Must we endure him for such time until we are settled in Virginia?"

"We shall." This was the voice of Captain Newport. "I've not seen reason to do anything other than that, Archer. He is a man of much knowledge of the sea. As prone as he is to try to tell others what to do, we need him."

"Indeed!" said Archer. "I've as much knowledge as Smith and my experience is as valuable or more so. Yet I don't scheme to overthrow us all when we've arrived in Virginia."

"I've not heard that kind of talk from Smith, either," said Newport. "Is your imagination heightened by our time at sea?"

"Not my imagination, sir, but my understanding of the conniving mind and the untrustworthy soul."

"I'll listen to this no more," said Newport. "I've work to do." There were footsteps across the deck to Newport's cabin at the stern of the ship.

Archer took a deep breath and blew it out noisily. He grumbled to himself. Then there was a whisper.

Nat glanced over his shoulder quickly. Kendall was there now, standing next to Archer. Both men's capes billowed like dark sails in the sea wind. The two were talking softly, and Nat couldn't hear what was being said. He looked back at the water and dropped a few more mice into the brine.

Then Archer said loudly, "There is the king himself!"

Curiosity took charge of Nat's feet and turned him around. At the center of the deck stood Kendall, Archer, and now Smith. Smith's chin was tipped upward and his hands were clenched at his sides. Surely, Nat thought, these men wouldn't resort to a brawl. That was something street urchins did, not captains.

Smith glanced at Richard and Nat. With a sharp jerk

of his head, he said, "You two. Below, the both of you."

Nat hesitated, and Smith shouted, "I said go now!"

Richard and Nat carried their buckets to the bow-side hatch. Richard scrambled down the ladder and dropped onto the floor. Nat followed, but halfway down, he stopped and climbed back up and peeked his head through the hatch.

Archer had his hand now on the hilt of his sword. Kendall's hand was on the dagger at his waist. Smith, feet planted apart with the rocking of the ship, still maintained clenched fists, but did not touch either of his weapons.

"Hail to our misguided lord!" said Archer. "The man who would crown himself king if chance presented itself."

"King Smith," said Kendall. "What a distasteful sound that is, and what a distasteful smell comes from his direction!"

"Sirs," said Smith. "I've never said I would be king. Do not lower yourselves by speaking in such a manner."

"Hah!" Archer's laugh was deep and without any humor. "You, sir, are the lowest. No one could lie upon this deck and be as low as you. The rats in the hold look down upon you, and the lice stay clear."

Smith's hand went to his sword. "Recant, sir."

"I will not take back the truth. I am not a liar."

"Recant your words or you will regret the moment they left your lips."

"I am not a liar!"

For a moment there was silence, except for the rush of the water and the call of sailors at the masts. Nat's hands trembled on the top ladder rung. The captains' hair and capes lifted and fell in the current of air, waving to each other in childlike taunts. The men stared hard and cold.

And then Smith drew his sword in a flash, and

jumped toward Archer with the point to the man's throat. Kendall brayed and skipped away. Archer's eyes went wide as moons.

"Recant," hissed Smith. "Or your words will be your death!"

Archer sputtered, clearly frightened. Then he managed, "No, sir. I'm afraid your actions here have only proven me correct."

"Nat!" called Richard from below. "Get down here!"

Nat waved frantically to keep Richard still.

Smith stepped up closer to Archer, keeping the point of the sword at the man's neck. There was a bead of blood where the blade touched. Smith's teeth were bared, his nostrils flaring. "Deny your words, Archer!"

But there was a shouting from the door to the Great Cabin. Newport stood, hat in his hands, his mouth open in fury. Slamming his hat onto his head, he hurried down the ladder and shoved Smith and Archer apart. "What is this? On my good ship I have one captain ready to take the life of another?"

Smith sheathed his sword and said, "I have cause, sir. If you'd only seen the behavior of these two, of Archer and Kendall, you'd know why I acted as I did."

But Archer threw his arms apart in a gesture of surprise. "I have no idea of which he speaks! The man charged me, unprovoked, and made to slit my throat!"

Kendall pushed from the side of the ship and stood by Archer. "It's true, my lord. Smith is rabid in his actions! The man would have murdered Archer had you not come upon us when you did. He must be taken into custody."

"Yes," said Archer. "Confine the man, that we might hang him when we reach the next island!"

But Smith stood straight and looked Newport directly in the eye. "Captain Newport, it was not without provocation that I pulled my sword. These two men have played their petty game of jealousy since we set sail from London."

Newport said, "Give me your weapons, Smith."

"Sir, these men called me names so foul that no man could tolerate such abuse!"

"We are innocent of such absurd charges," said Archer. "Foul names? His mind plays tricks on him. You saw his actions. We have no option but to put the man in chains."

Newport shook his head in resignation. "Smith, give me your weapons. I will have a court of inquiry tomorrow, but for now, you must be secured in your cabin."

Smith stared angrily between Archer and Kendall, but then reluctantly handed his dagger and sword to Newport.

"He should be put into the galley, Captain Newport," said Archer. "What punishment is it that he be allowed to stay in his own cabin, where I myself must sleep?"

"Sleep elsewhere, then, until court is held," said Newport. "But until he is found guilty, he will not go into the galley."

Newport then gestured to the door to Smith's cabin. Kendall and Archer glanced at each other. Then Archer said, "Will you not at least bind the man? He is a danger, sir, you saw it with your very eyes!"

"Not until the court!" said Newport. "Now I will speak no more of this until morning."

Nat watched as Newport put Smith into his cabin. Then the captain called to a sailor and spoke with him quietly. The sailor stood, arms crossed, outside Smith's door. Clearly the cabin was to be guarded until court was held.

Someone tugged on Nat's shoe, and he looked down. It was Edward Brookes. The man was holding a waste bucket. "Make yourself useful, boy," he said.

"There are three more buckets ready to be emptied. Now, be quick!"

That night, when Nat lay down to sleep, his mind wouldn't let go of what he'd seen. He pulled out his paper, flattened the rumples from the surface, and uncapped the ink. He wrote,

If Archer and Kendall knew I saw the truth. If they realized that I saw the provocation Smith was subjected to, they would throw me into the sea like a pan of vomit.

He rolled onto his side and tucked his hand beneath his head and shivered. Then he wrote,

What will happen in the court of inquiry tomorrow? If Smith is found innocent, all will be well, except that Archer and Kendall will continue to make their trouble. But if Smith is found guilty, he will be confined in the hold, down with the vermin and the stench of the bilge. And when we reach land, he will surely be hanged.

When Nat went to sleep at last, he dreamed of a rope about his neck and men laughing at him. He was being hoisted up to mizzenmast to the great blue sky, unable to breathe.

He clutched at his throat and screamed as the rope grew tighter and tighter.

Nat's legs kicked out as his vision shattered; he found himself in the blackness of the 'tween deck, lying on a thin, straw-stuffed mattress.

He sat up. His hands went instantly to his neck, and he was relieved to find the dream noose gone. He wondered if he had called out in his sleep, but no one around seemed disturbed, not even the irritable Samuel Collier.

Nat lay back down and linked his fingers beneath his head. Maybe he hadn't yelled, but he was surprised that the dreadfully loud hammering of his heart hadn't startled any of the gentlemen out of their mysterious, mindless sleeps.

❦ 5 ❦

March 21, 1607

THE COURT OF inquiry was held out on the upper deck, and only gentlemen were allowed to attend. Nat paced the 'tween deck, rolling his pebbles in his palms, wondering if he should go up the ladder and tell what he had seen. They certainly couldn't hang Smith if they knew the truth of the incident. Surely Newport was a man concerned with truth and fairness.

But in spite of the taunting dream, he knew it was best to say nothing. To play the idiot.

Richard was curious about what was going on up the ladder, but he didn't let on. He was weaving a small mat with some loose straw he'd found, bending over it and pretending to be intensely content to be at this task.

Samuel sat on his pallet, driven to distraction by Nat's pacing.

"Sit down, urchin," he commanded. "With so much back and forth you'll tip the ship over and we'll all drown."

"Tell the lapdog to be silent, Nat," said Richard, looking up from his weaving.

"I will not be silent," said Samuel. "I am free and I may speak as I wish."

Nat took a breath and blew it out through his teeth.

Then there were men's voices and footsteps on the ladder. Nat's hands found each other and made a single, tight fist.

It was a pair of sailors, who squinted about and then gazed at Nat.

"You, boy!" called one sailor. "You are the one!"

"Me?" asked Nat. His heart pounded in anticipation.

"You are called for to speak at the inquiry!" said the sailor.

Dear God! Nat thought. *Someone knows I was watching! Who could it have been? What am I to say? What is to happen?*

"What're ya waiting for, get up here now!"

Nat glanced at Richard and Samuel, who were both watching with the same stunned expression. Then he followed the sailors up the ladder and to the Great Cabin at the stern of the ship.

He'd never been inside this room and had never expected to be. Whatever cleaning or vermin extermination was done for Captain Newport was handled by one of the sailors. It was not a large space compared to the width and breadth of the 'tween deck, but it had a feeling of light and grandeur. There were two oak cots against either side, with a desk covered in rolled charts, instruments, pens, and inkwells, a cabinet for clothing, a shelf for books, and several lanterns hanging on brass hooks. Small square windows revealed the sea to either side, and they allowed in plenty of sunlight, enough for men to see during this daytime hour without lighting the lanterns.

But it was crowded this morning. Men stood in tight clusters, all facing the side of the room where Captain Smith stood in his shackles. Newport was at the desk, hands folded, clearly exasperated yet keeping his emotions in check. Archer was up, pacing as best he could in the cramped quarters. This inquiry had been going on for over an hour now.

Nat was shoved against the wall by the door, behind Kendall and Edward Brookes. Most of the men in the cabin didn't seem to notice he had been brought in, and the few who did gave him disdainful glances.

"Mutiny," Archer was saying. "The man is clearly up to it. It is clear he's planned it from the beginning. Smith has no respect for those in command, such as yourself, Captain Newport. He sees himself as the dashing rogue, hero to the underlings such as the sailors, commoners, and laborers, winning their favor for his own gain."

"Untrue," said Smith simply.

Archer pointed a finger at Smith, close enough to brush the other's nose. Smith did not flinch. "Look at your own history, Smith. Fighting with the Hungarians for adventure, not for the good of England but for your own glory, I daresay! Caught and sold as a slave by the Turks, escaping to Russia and then home again, full of tales which catch the fancy of those who listen. But if they listened more carefully and more deeply, they would see what we see, nothing but a braggart after his own interests."

"Yes!" echoed several other gentlemen.

Archer continued, "I daresay you were never taken slave but conjured the elaborate tale to make yourself into somewhat of a legend! And you see the opportunity to be legend yet again, at the expense of the Virginia Company!"

"I was provoked into the fight with you," said Smith. "I would not raise my sword but for the same reason you would, sir. To protect the honor of my name. If I was unshackled at this moment, I would raise it again for what lies you have said against me just now."

"Indeed!" said Newport at his desk.

"I care for the welfare of this expedition as much as the next," said Smith. "I have said it before and will say it again, it is your jealousy speaking. You wish you had but a fraction of the courage I have!"

"Arrogance!" said Archer.

"Truth," said Smith.

Captain Newport shook his head, then his gaze fell upon Nat. "There is the boy you requested, Smith."

God save me!

"Boy," said Captain Newport, one eyebrow raised beneath his cap. "Smith has made a request that you be brought in to tell what you saw on the deck yesterday."

"Me?" Nat was shocked that he could find his voice. "What I saw, sir?"

Smith looked at Nat straight on, and in an even tone said, "You witnessed the altercation from the onset, boy, did you not?"

"I . . . ," began Nat.

"You were on the ladder, making for the 'tween deck, but you stopped, and I saw you watching there. I am not a successful warrior nor—" he gave Archer a quick, cold glance "—a cunning man who escaped the clutches of Turkish slavery because I do not observe what is about me. And I observed you, boy. On the ladder. Tell these fine gentlemen what you saw."

"Well, sir . . . ," said Nat.

"Of course he will testify on behalf of Smith," said Kendall, giving Nat a shove and knocking him against the door. "This smelly little hold mouse? That is what Smith is hoping for, to win the affections of the common folks so they will do his bidding!"

"So they will lie for him," said Archer.

"Regardless," said Captain Newport. "Boy, have your

say. You have been called to testify as to what you observed yesterday from the ladder."

What do I say? Nat thought frantically. *If I speak on behalf of Smith, I am in danger of the others. If I speak on behalf of Archer, I am in danger of Smith.*

"Speak!" demanded Newport.

"The sun was in my eyes, sir," said Nat. "So brightly I could not tell a cloud from a sail. I saw nothing."

"No?" said Newport. "Then tell us what you heard."

"There were several men below me on the 'tween deck who were in a row, so loud a row that I could make out nothing but the argument. I heard not a word spoken between Captain Archer and Captain Smith." Nat did not look at Smith, but at the floor. It was a nice floor, even and covered with a piece of Oriental rug.

"Ah," said Newport. "Then take the boy back where he belongs. That was a waste of our time!"

A soldier grabbed Nat by the upper arm and steered him out through the door. Nat was left on his own to go back down to the 'tween deck.

Richard nearly pounced on Nat, tossing his weaving aside. "What happened?"

"Nothing," said Nat as he plopped onto his pallet.

"What did you say?"

"I said nothing. I had nothing to say."

"Damn you!"

"So be it."

Nat drew up his knees and waited. It was another hour before there was word from above. Edward Brookes clambered down the ladder and wiped his hands in satisfaction.

"Well," he said as he pointed a finger in Samuel's direction. "You are no longer a page. You are now a laborer like these other two boys. We'll have you killing rats and dumping our pails."

Samuel was incredulous. "No longer a page?"

Edward Brookes giggled. He dabbed at his face with a dainty, chubby finger. "Smith has been found guilty of attempting murder and mutiny. He is confined in the galley, and will not be allowed out until we stop for more supplies. There, we will hang him by his neck until he is dead."

"Guilty?" Samuel's word was barely a whisper.

"Yes," said Archer, who was just now coming down the ladder. "Praise God justice has prevailed. The man will hang and we will all be the better for it."

"And I am to clean the waste buckets and kill vermin?"

"Unless you want to hang like your master for disobeying the order of a gentleman," said Edward Brookes. He rubbed at a fold of fat beneath his chin. "You'll do exactly as you are told."

Samuel went silent. The gentlemen, clearly pleased for the most part with the verdict, settled down and picked up their dice and their cards and their flutes. The commoners drew together and whispered in disappointed voices.

"Nat," said Richard. "Smith is going to hang."

"Yes."

"We'll have no one to take our part should things get bad! He was the only one who treated us as men."

"I know."

"There must be something we can do!"

"Absolutely not. We must continue as we have."

"But, Nat, he will hang!"

"I am sorry for Smith. But what I feel matters not at all. I should just as well believe the sun should be purple, and the waters of the ocean filled with cattle to be caught and brought a-deck for our meals."

"You do not care?"

"I can't care. And neither can you."

"If you were unjustly sentenced for an imagined infraction," said Richard, "I would come to your part!"

"If it was life or death, you would not. And I would not for you, either. Now, be quiet. The men are listening to us."

Richard went silent. Nat could feel the confusion and anger steaming off him. But Nat couldn't change the facts. Smith was a survivor. If anyone could escape a hanging, this man could. And if not, then there was nothing Nat could do about it. He and Richard needed to survive, too, and on this cursed ship it would take a blind eye and deaf ear to accomplish that.

6

April 19, 1607

Smith is a survivor! I can learn much from watching him.
We sailed along the islands of the West Indies days ago and
disembarked on several occasions to replenish supplies of food
and water. We stayed three days on one lush tropical isle
named Nevis.

Archer told us, "Here we shall wash our clothes and ourselves. We shall eat good foods of this place and recover our
strength. Then we shall take care of our prisoner and leave
his body like carrion for the scavenging natives!"

"Ah," said Edward Brookes. "Entertainment for us all."

Richard, Samuel, and I were compelled to carry several gentlemen's goods up the ladder, but when we got out on deck,
we found soldiers, gentlemen, and captains alike staring in
amazement over the railing at the shore.

John Smith was standing on the sandy beach, alone. He
was in full uniform, with his helmet in place, breast armor
on, and cape swept back, showing his sword, dagger, and
powder horn. From his boot top protruded yet another, smaller
dagger. In one hand was a musket. Smith was smiling as if
to say, "Come and get me, any who dare!"

Archer shook his fist. "How did that man get ashore? How
did he gain access to weapons?"

Kendall shouted, "Who helped this murderous villain gain transportation to the shore?"

No one answered. Each man seemed as confused as the other. The pinnace had been lowered into the water already, so clearly someone had rowed the captain ashore.

I couldn't imagine who had done this, but was glad.

Archer complained angrily to Newport as the gentlemen took their turns being rowed to the beach. The pinnaces from the Discovery and Godspeed also carried their passengers to the banks of the island, although once on the land, no one went to take hold of John Smith. Instead, everyone stood back and watched as Smith settled himself on the ground with a few curious, naked natives who had come from the forest, and tried to hold conversation with them.

Richard and I were in the last shuttle. As I climbed down into the pinnace, I heard Archer tell Newport on deck, "The carpenter Edward Pising will bring tools. There is wood here. We will carry out Smith's sentence in spite of his trickery."

The sand on the island was warm. Sailors brought the store of weapons ashore. Even Richard, Samuel, and I were outfitted with helmets and muskets. Once everyone was off the ships and gathered around, we knelt while Reverend Hunt blessed the land and the ships and the voyage.

"Protect us and let us carry Your glory into this land," Hunt prayed.

Then everyone stood and looked again at John Smith.

Archer said, "We will now build a gallows for Smith!"

But Newport said, "Indeed? I have decided I will not go after Smith. See how quickly he has made friends of the savages yonder? He is invaluable. Leave him be."

Archer was incredulous. "Leave him be? We held court and he is condemned to die! Kendall, support what I say."

Captain Kendall came and stood beside Archer, but the eye he kept on Smith showed hesitation.

Reverend Hunt then approached Newport and the other two captains and said quietly, "God may have His hand in this.

Smith has befriended the savages, blessing our presence with peace rather than war."

"I cannot believe my ears!" shouted Archer.

"Do you mean to confront him, then?" asked Newport. "Go ahead, Archer, if you feel you cannot face another day without hanging John Smith!"

Archer glared at Smith, who had stood now and had turned again to face the company of men. The wind tossed his cape; the smile on his face was defiant and confident.

"Face him and his talents with sword and dagger," said Newport. "But you and Kendall will do it alone, for I will have nothing to do with the man's death."

Archer stared at Smith for another moment, then spun on his heel and stalked away. Kendall trotted after.

With Newport's unofficial pardon of Smith's conviction, we all went about exploration. We journeyed inland and found a large, warm spring which was just the proper temperature for long and soothing baths. Smith was back in the fold; he chatted with a number of the men and laughed with others, while Archer, Kendall, and their close friends scowled uselessly.

Days later we sailed west to an equally lovely island of the West Indies called Mona. It was here, on April 7th, that we lost the gentleman Edward Brookes on a lush green hillside. A long hike proved too much. I heard the gentleman George Percy explain to another that Brookes's fat melted inside him and he died. I learned much from the sniveling Brookes. I learned what type of man I will never become, regardless of the wealth I gain in Virginia.

We are on our ships again, with no more stops between here and Virginia. Samuel has grown melancholy and quiet. Even with his master out of chains, he seems as if he's lost some of his nastiness. I think I liked him better when he was obnoxious. At least, he was more interesting.

Soon we will be there. Soon.

Soon I shall walk barefoot in the gold I have come to know so intimately in my dreams. I shall build my home and send for servants from London to work for me, to tend my animals and raise my garden and stand guard over my treasures. I will be strong like John Smith, and cunning, and quick. I will never be cold again. I will never be poor again. I will never be hungry again.

The time is so close. The time of suffering is nearly done! Thank God.

❧ 7. ❧

April 26, 1607

"VIRGINIA!" Nat's eyes opened.

"It is there!" came the shout from up deck. "The shores of Virginia, and it is as good and fair a land as we have ever seen!"

Everyone went up to the deck and stared. Nat wormed his way beneath shoulders and elbows to the railing.

Virginia! We have made it!

"Praise God from whom all blessings are bestowed!" said Reverend Hunt.

"Amen!" shouted the men. Above, on the roundtops, sailors cheered and howled in the pale morning light.

Nat turned his face to the breeze and took a long breath of the Virginia coastal air. The three ships sailed more closely to the land and dropped their anchors. The pinnaces were lowered and made ready to carry some of the men ashore. Across the water, there was visible a beautiful land, different from England and Mona but lovely in its own right. Sparkling sand, waving waterside plants, and tall needle-leaved and broad-leaved trees stood back from the beach like watchful citizens.

"Cape Henry," said John Smith as he stood near Nat and nodded at the land. "We shall name that fine point of land Cape Henry in honor of the Prince of Wales."

No one argued or disputed this name, because although Nat could tell by some of the gentlemen's expressions that they wouldn't have cared for any name suggested by Smith, it seemed the right thing to do on behalf of the prince.

The pinnace set off to the shore. Newport sat at the helm, and behind him were Smith, Archer, and Kendall and several sailors and soldiers. The *Godspeed* and *Discovery* also launched their small boats filled with explorers. Nat could see from his vantage place on the ship's deck there were two boys on the *Godspeed*'s pinnace. Nat envied them; they would be among the first to step on Virginia's soil. The small boats reached the shore and the men climbed out and ventured over a sandy knoll where they could no longer be seen.

"I would like to be with them," said Nat to Richard. "I imagine I could be a good soldier here. I told Smith that I was a soldier."

"Just act as a soldier and you shall be one," said Richard.

Nat laughed. "You're learning!"

Suddenly the carpenter Edward Pising grabbed Nat by the arm and said, "We have some repairs from the last storm. You boys come with me." Nat and Richard spent the next hours driving nails into loosened boards all around the upper deck and in the cabins.

When the afternoon shadows grew long, the workers took a break, munching handfuls of hardtack and prunes and drinking their allotted beer. Nat ate quickly, knowing soon they would have better food from the land of Virginia. No longer would he have to worry about saving a stale biscuit.

Then Edward Pising dropped his biscuit, tilted his head, and squinted in the direction of the shore. "Listen," he said.

Richard and Nat listened. There was a faint sound above that of the slapping waves, something like singing, high-pitched and resonant.

"What is that?" Nat wondered aloud.

Then they could hear that it was not singing at all but screams. From over the sandy knoll rushed the Englishmen. They ran in sheer terror, struggling in the sand, muskets held high. Some were yelling, others shouting. They jumped into the pinnaces and frantic sailors splashed knee-deep as they pushed the boats off into the deeper water.

"Lord save us!" said Edward Pising. "Savages!" Breaking from the scrubby vegetation and racing down after the men were several natives. They carried bows and arrows, and as they ran they set the bows straight and aimed at the retreating men.

"Watch out!" screamed Richard.

"Lay low!" cried the carpenter.

The natives drew back on their bows and released. Arrows arced in the air, coming down in a rain over the men of the *Susan Constant*'s pinnace.

Some arrows missed and fell into the water. Several others struck men in shoulders and arms. A sailor, now waist-deep in the water, struggling to climb aboard, was struck in the back and went down. Newport pulled him onto the boat by his shirt collar.

"Row!" cried Nat. Sailors hopped in with the others, and men frantically tugged the oars to steer the boats back to the mother ships. Smith stood straight in the small boat, gesturing wildly with his arms, shouting and directing the others. Archer stood up as well, as if even in this desperate situation, he could not let Smith take command.

On the beach, the natives lined arrows on their bowstrings and aimed again at the pinnaces. They let the arrows fly. Archer spun to face the beach, and his hands flew up in front of his face as he saw the arrows flying at him.

And then he screamed.

An arrow pierced his hands, one in front of the other, pinning them together. Archer fell backward into the boat. Another man grabbed the arrow and tore it free of Archer's hands. Archer screamed again.

"Row!" cried men from the deck of the *Susan Constant.*

Newport was at the stern of the boat then, legs planted apart to keep from tipping over. He raised his musket at the natives, who were yet again reloading their bows. He pulled on the trigger. The blast was loud and smoky, and the natives stopped midload to stare wide-eyed at the weapon pointed in their direction. But they shot arrows again, and again, men in the pinnaces were hit. Cries filled the air. Richard put his hands over his ears.

More men loaded the muskets with powder and ammunition, readied them, then fired across the waves at the attackers. Natives at last turned, and with loud wails and shouts, ran back over the sandy knoll and disappeared.

The boats were quickly rowed the rest of the distance to their ships, and the men, wounded and unhurt, were hauled up to the deck.

Men crowded about and had to be shoved back by the captains and the sailors. The man who had been shot in the back was severely wounded. The arrow still protruded from his body, and there was a second one in his thigh. It took two men and much effort to pull the bloody sticks from him.

"Be strong, Matthew Morton," said the sailor who held the arrow and then broke it in half angrily.

John Smith, sweating and rumpled but not wounded, said, "You took an arrow for us. That shows goodly faith and courage."

Matthew Morton clutched his belly and groaned as the blood ran through his fingers.

This is not acting, Nat thought. *This is truly a brave man. Could I be so brave?*

Morton was carried carefully and respectfully into the galley by two other sailors.

Captain Archer sat on the deck by the center hatch, making a great deal of noise.

"I am mortally wounded!" he shrieked. "My hands are so badly pierced I shall surely die!" Nat could see the holes in the hands, welling with red blood, coursing down his wrists in thick rivulets. His shirtsleeves were soaked.

The surgeon said, "Be still, and we shall do what we can." He motioned for help, and Archer was lifted to his feet and taken to Newport's cabin.

Newport stayed on deck, clearly undeterred by the attack. "We shall wait a short time before we return," he said. "The savages know our power, they will not likely attack again soon. Tomorrow morning we shall go ashore and assemble the shallop. Tomorrow we shall explore. Tomorrow we shall bless Virginia in the name of God and the king."

Gentlemen and commoners alike nodded in agreement. And then Newport said, "And now, as instructed, we shall open the box in which is listed the council for Virginia. We shall know who is to be the leaders in our new land."

Gentlemen and commoners nodded again, but this

time it was clear they nodded for different reasons. Gentlemen hoped they would find the council list to their liking, and that John Smith would not be part. Sailors, soldiers, and laborers hoped that Smith would be on the list.

Newport, Smith, and several other gentlemen went to Newport's cabin. With a pleased tossing of his head and winking in Richard's direction, Samuel Collier followed. Captains from the other ships were hailed and invited to come onto the *Susan Constant* to hear the reading. They came in their pinnaces, which were tethered to the *Susan Constant*'s side. The men came aboard and without a word, went to the Great Cabin.

No one wanted to go below. Everyone wanted to know who was on the list. There was small talk to pass the time. Richard leaned against the ship's railing by Nat and said, "I do not think Smith will make the list. He was charged with attempted murder and found guilty."

"The list was made before we left," Nat said. "I think Smith will be included. And I'll wager my first piece of Virginia gold that I'm right."

The night sky grew dark, and stars made their twinkling appearances overhead. Everyone was restless. How long did it take to open a box and read names? But at last the door to the Great Cabin swung wide and Newport came out. His face was set in a serious mood and it was impossible for Nat to tell from that expression if Smith was in or out. Newport held a piece of rolled paper.

"We have our council," Newport said simply. "These are the men who will share in the leadership of the Virginia colony."

It was as though everyone on deck took a breath at the same time. "Christopher Newport," said Newport, and there were murmurs of agreement. "Edward Maria

Wingfield, Bartholomew Gosnold, John Ratcliffe, John Martin, George Kendall." Then Newport clenched his fist. He glanced back over his shoulder to the Great Cabin where the other men still tarried and then out at the men on the deck. Then Newport said no more, turned and went inside.

"I heard there were to be seven councilors," said Edward Pising. "He read only six."

"I do not understand," said a gentleman. "But I am glad Smith was not on the list!"

Everyone retired below deck.

Richard punched the side of his mattress to soften it a bit and said, "You owe me your first gold."

Nat didn't answer.

It wasn't long before Samuel Collier came below. He looked drawn and tired and upset. Nat didn't want to speak to the boy, but curiosity overcame dislike. "What happened in the Cabin that had Newport looking so troubled?"

Samuel dropped to his mattress and took off his hat. "John Smith was on the list."

"What?" asked Nat.

"He was on the list, but the other councilors say they will not seat him. Wingfield and Kendall were the most adamant in their objections. They convinced the others that Smith would be bad for the colony. They said he had selfish interests. Smith agreed to abide by their decision temporarily. Somehow, he will show them he is fit to council. But not for now." The boy then lay down and went silent.

"I will take your first-found pearl if you would rather keep the gold," Nat said to Richard with a laugh.

Richard grumbled softly and rolled over to sleep. Nat looked at the blackness of the 'tween deck ceiling. Smith was on the council. This would be a good thing for himself. Smith could be counted on. Smith, at least, didn't see Richard and Nat as less than human.

8

May 12, 1607

The past days have been filled with excitement and work. We all went onshore, armed and helmeted, ready for adventure. But I found adventure is, for now, the privilege of others, not common boys. The first act was to give thanks to God for His mercy. Laborers cut down a tree and constructed a large cross. It was erected on the beach of Cape Henry, and the Reverend Hunt gave a long oration on God's anger and power. We knelt in the damp sand and prayed. Seabirds circled overhead, and I thought I could hear a distant chanting of savages and pulsing of drums.

I sense they are anxious we are here. They do not want us taking their mountains of gold. I would not want anyone taking my gold, either, but these are people who are not even Christians, and I've heard gentlemen say that God doesn't reward those who do not worship Him properly.

After our prayer, we stood, and the mood shifted to anticipation. Gentlemen and soldiers gathered together to explore the cape. They left us commoners behind to assemble the shallop. I wanted to explore so very much! I have suffered the journey on the ship as well as any of the others! But I had to keep my thoughts to myself.

I have finished my midday meal, and in moment—

"Boy!" came a sharp voice. It was one of the carpenters in charge of putting the boat together. "Put that dabbling away, you've done with your meal now back to work!"

Nat cursed under his breath and slipped the pen and paper into the front of his shirt. Then he stood and went back to work on the shallop.

The shallop was a boat larger than a pinnace, made of wood brought from London and constructed on the very sands of Cape Henry. It would be used to carry twenty-five men up rivers to investigate. The wood was already measured and cut, so that all the workers had to do was fit it together.

Nat, Richard, and a boy named Nicholas Skot from the *Godspeed* had been put to this task, helping lay out the wood and hold planks in place while Edward Pising ordered them and the other laborers about. Samuel Collier had been allowed to go inland with the explorers, carrying supplies for John Smith.

"Where is the other boy?" Nat asked Nicholas as they stood side by side with a curved length of wood as nails were driven in. "Was there not a boy your size, named James or John? I saw him at the spring on the island of Mona."

Nicholas said, "James Brumfield. He was killed."

Richard's eyes went wide. "Killed? How? When?"

"He went ashore yesterday with the others in the pinnace, and was pierced by an arrow."

"Were you on the pinnace, too?" Richard asked.

Nicholas nodded. "We both were on the expedition ashore. It was fine for a while. And then . . ." He paused. His eyes tightened. "Then there were the shouts, the arrows, and then James was cut through. I tried to hold the blood in his chest, but it poured out so dreadfully fast. I couldn't push the life back in, though God knows I tried."

"Here! Hold the plank still!" shouted Edward Pising. "Be quiet and pay attention. We must have this right!"

The work went well into the late afternoon. Nat held planks as still as possible and watched Edward Pising carefully. This work was hard. The man's hands were scarred and tough as weathered wood. Nat knew he would be responsible for helping build once they settled; then, of course, he would find gold and pay for another boy to come to Virginia and do his work for him.

A sailor smacked Nat soundly on the head, jostling him out of his thoughts. "We're done with this plank. What do you think? We will now let you sit down for tea? Come to this side now and make yourself of some worth!"

The shallop was done by nightfall, and the gentlemen returned from their exploring and sat about the fire, talking and laughing as the stars traveled their course.

The following morning, as Nat restoked the fire with wood he had collected earlier, Newport selected men to take the shallop on an exploration up the wide river to find a site for the permanent colony.

John Smith did not look at all bothered that he had been banned from his seat on the council. In fact, he was as animated and excited as ever. His cape flapped like a seabird's wing, and his face was flushed with intensity. He came over to where Nathaniel and Richard stood eating hardtack beneath a brine-weathered tree and said, "You, Richard Mutton. You look strong enough to make an expedition and small enough to take up just a little space. You seem fit and quick. A few of our older soldiers are still recovering from the savage attack. Although my friend Archer is going with us, his wounded hands will not be much good for a number of days yet. We need another armed man."

Richard looked from Smith to Nat and back to Smith. "Yes, sir," he said.

"But . . ." began Nat. "But, sir, I am stronger and bigger, as you can well see. Do you remember in London? I told you I was a soldier!"

Smith held up a hand. "This time Richard will go with us. You will have another chance."

Richard looked uncertainly at Nat, then followed Smith down the beach to the shallop, where men were placing arms and bundles. Samuel Collier was with them, wearing his feathered hat, holding Smith's personal items. Soon everyone was settled. With a splash of the oars, they pushed off and headed northwest.

Nat stood alone, holding on to a thin branch of the tree, watching as the shallop vanished. *Curses!* he thought.

There was work to do, and Nat threw himself into it. There were oysters and other shellfish to gather from the shallows, wood to gather to keep the fire burning, and with a stream nearby, clothing to wash.

Every so often, Nat would steal a glance of Nicholas Skot. He stopped himself several times from speaking to the boy, reminding himself of his own decision to remain aloof. If he made it here in Virginia, he would make it without sentiment, without pity. It was too bad that Nicholas was mourning his friend. What good would that do him?

The shallop was gone a very long time. One day ran into another, and even though Nat had enough to do to keep busy, he found himself frequently stopping and staring out across the river and wondering how long the shallop would be gone. Had they run into trouble at the hands of the natives? Was Smith still alive? What adventure was Richard discovering? Did he already have a pocketful of gold? Jealously made the backs of Nat's arms hot.

While putting mussels into a pot on the fire, Nat listened to the conversation of Jehu Robinson and another man who were seated nearby on the sand. "It is May eleventh already," said Jehu. "The shallop has been gone many days. I wonder if bad fate has befallen them."

The other man, older with a blistering face and clearly a commoner, said, "Whom did they take but gentlemen and a handful of soldiers? Gentlemen! Men who went only to be seers of sights. They have no skill in arms, save a prissy duel, and they have not the brawn to do battle at arm's length. It could well be that at this moment, John Smith is rowing the lot of them, dead bodies all, back to Cape Henry. And thus the delay."

Jehu said, "You might well be right."

The older man nodded. "They could have taken me. I am strong and could outwit any gentlemen on our expedition. I do so dislike gentlemen, and this trip has not given me reason to change my attitude. Well, sir, except for you."

Jehu smiled.

Nat stirred up the mussels and went back down the beach to dig for more. Perhaps, he thought, he might just turn up some Virginia pearls for his effort. This was the land of riches, after all.

It was another two days before the shallop came into view on the river. Nat was glad to see the boat, but what if the old commoner was right and there were dead men there, rowed by battered captains? But as the shallop neared the shore and a sailor jumped out to pull it in closer, Nat saw that every man was there, and safe. They talked nonstop with each other; they carried strange items of feathers and fur, obviously given them by natives.

Richard's complexion was ruddy now, and as he hopped from the shallop and waded through the water to the beach, Nat thought he even seemed taller.

"Tell me!" Nat said, grabbing his arm. "What have you seen, Richard? What did you find? Gold? You brought me some, surely!"

But Richard held up a finger, nodding toward Captain Newport, who had pulled his hat from his bald head, tucked it beneath his arm, and stood before the fire with his hands spread as if ready to make a proclamation. "We have found many riches here in Virginia," the captain said. "There are natives who welcomed us with friendliness. They laid down their arrows and bows, and there were celebrations and dancing on our behalf. Chiefs or presidents, called *weroances,* of many tribes greeted us with signs of peace, and we were served in a manner most fair."

"And what riches have you found?" asked Edward Pising. "Have you gold hiding in your pockets?"

But Newport shook his head. "Our riches have been the peace with which we have been greeted by the natives of Virginia. And the land which is rich for growing crops, and the fresh waters in streams and ponds all about."

Many of the gentlemen who had not gone on the shallop frowned. Nat gave Richard a questioning glance. Richard nodded solemnly, affirming what Newport had said.

"No gold yet?" said one gentleman. "Surely it is not deep in the ground that we must dig for it?"

"Surely you were not looking carefully," said another. "Fear of natives kept you from watching your steps and certainly you trod on top of the gold without knowing it!"

"We will sail our ships in the morning to find our

settlement site," Newport said. "Get a good sleep tonight."

The men set several new fires, and around these they all gathered and fell into sleep, with only the watch keeping eyes open for natives or wild animals.

Nat, Richard, and Nicholas Skot sat in the cold sand, and once again Nat interrogated Richard.

"Tell me what you saw," he said. "I should have gone and so you owe it to me to tell me what you discovered."

Richard sat with his legs crossed, looking toward the fire several yards away. He seemed older. Even his voice sounded a bit different, deeper maybe, more adult. But his enthusiasm hadn't waned.

"There is a river, I cannot say how long it is," he began, the light from the fire dancing in his eyes. "It may reach the East India Sea, some of the men believe. Thick trees and flowers line the way, with tributaries from deep within the forests. Birds and animals drank along the river, such as I've never seen before. Some animals had no fur on their tails; making them look like rats, yet not rats. Others were so quick, I couldn't see anything but a flash of teeth and claws!"

"And the riches?" said Nicholas. "Newport said you found none, but surely you picked up something!"

"We met many savages, frightful but curious. As Captain Newport said, they gave us meat and drink, some tasty, some foul. They danced and performed for us."

"And what of the savages' gold?" asked Nat. "Did you spy it in a tent? Do they wearing it around their necks?"

"I saw no gold."

"None at all?" asked Nat.

"No," said Richard. "But I don't doubt it is here. We'll find it, don't worry."

"I hope so," said Nicholas.

"We will," said Richard.

"We will," said Nat, stretching out to sleep. "I'm not concerned. We will find it in good time. All in good time."

❧ 9 ❧

May 13–19, 1607

"A T LAST," CAPTAIN Archer said, standing on deck with the bandages still on his hands and a small but rare smile on his face. "Such will be our new home."

The *Susan Constant,* the *Godspeed,* and the *Discovery* had traveled all day, sailing up the broad river, which had been named the James in honor of the king of England, and as the shadows had begun to grow long over the river, the place of settlement was found. It was a wooded peninsula, lush and inviting. There seemed to be no native villages nearby. The water was deep enough close to shore that the sailors threw out ropes and moored the ships to the trees. It was decided to wait until morning to unload to have benefit of sunlight to get a fortress up as quickly as possible.

And morning came very early. Before even a hint of light had filtered down into the 'tween deck, there was noise and movement on the upper deck. Everyone rose quickly and made ready to disembark. First, however, they would all attend the swearing in of the new council.

All the gentlemen who had been named to the council came onto the deck of the *Susan Constant*, and a vote was taken by the members to choose a president. Although Nat was certain Captain Newport would be the one, it was a man Nat didn't know, Edward Maria Wingfield. Nat watched John Smith as the oaths were taken and an oration given. The captain seemed to be in his own world, glancing between the new council members and the shore. His eyes were bright with ideas and his head tilted on occasion as if he were listening carefully to his own thoughts.

The sun was fully up now, and the gentlemen took their personal items across the plank to the place they had named James Towne. Sailors unloaded the barrels and crates, hauling smaller ones out through the cannon hatches on the ships' sides, hoisting the others through the center hatches with ropes. The pigs and chickens and goats were unusually noisy as if they knew they were, at last, home.

Nat balanced himself across the plank from ship to shore. The paper he had stolen from Samuel was rolled up and tucked into his waistband at his hip. He touched it tentatively. He'd have to find a place to hide this. Pulling his fur hat down over his ears, he jumped from the plank to the land. The ground was soft and damp.

Laborers grabbed axes and hatches and immediately began to fell trees to split into planks for a church and a fortress. Soon additional wood would be cut into clapboard cargo to be sent back to England when Newport returned later in the summer. Some sailors returned to the ships to look the vessels over again and, from the sounds of laughter and singing Nat heard from shore, to enjoy some of the remaining beer and whisky in celebration. The tents, smelling of mold and filled with rot-holes, were pitched and patched for use until cottages could be constructed. The work went on for many days.

Richard and Nat were assigned the task of stripping branches from trees felled by the larger men. A disgruntled Samuel Collier had been put to work dragging logs alongside Nicholas Skot. As Nat worked, he watched for the opportunity to speak with John Smith. Nat wanted to go on an expedition like Richard had. It was his turn. He wanted to be scouting instead of slinging an axe. He wanted to learn about the forests and the streams and the dangers in Virginia. He wanted to be able to come back and sketch his own maps for his own use later on. Nat knew it would be a little while before he could actually search for gold— only mindless gentlemen would think gold was the first item necessary for living in this wilderness—but when he had a home and food and a knowledge of the land, he would then go out on his own and find his fortune.

Virginia was a curious place. The trees were stately and wide, and of kinds that Nat had never seen. The animals that peeked from the forest were strange enough to cause one to pause and look. Once such animal was like the stag hunted in England, but it had a softer face and a tail that flashed white when it was startled. Another animal was short and black with a white stripe down its flat back. Nicholas Skot had tried to catch one such animal several days earlier and had been sprayed with an essence so foul he was forced to bathe several times in the water of the James before he was tolerable again. The stink lingered several days. Virginia's weather was pleasant, with temperatures comfortable enough to work without heavy outer layers.

"Do you remember telling Smith you knew how to do this?" Richard asked Nat on an early morning as he chopped branches from a downed tree. His shirt was tied at his waist. Nat's was on a rock. Several hundred feet away, other men were pulling planks into upright positions to fashion the walls of the fort. "We were standing on the street in London. A lifetime ago!"

"I remember," said Nat. "Aren't you glad you listened to me, little man? We will be rich gentlemen soon."

Richard nodded exuberantly. "My arms hurt from this work, but that is all right. I shall hope that Smith finds me worthy to once again go scouting. It was most amazing, Nat! You cannot imagine until you do it yourself. Meeting natives, tasting of their food, watching their pagan ceremonies as they welcomed us. Terrifying but incredible."

Nat swiped at a fly buzzing in his ear, feeling the burn of jealously rise up the back of his neck once more.

"I should want to take another trip up the river," said Richard. "Farther on this time—"

"Richard, say no more about your trip up the river. You've told me time and again, and I've grown more than weary of it."

But Richard did not hear the tone in Nat's voice, or he didn't care. "Farther on, and who knows what we might find? It makes me shiver to think of it, but not from fear but from excitement. If only—"

Nat had let go of his axe before Richard could utter another word, and had slammed his fists into his friend's chest, sending him flying to the ground with a "whoof!"

"Enough!" Nat said, bearing down on Richard with all his weight, causing the smaller boy to cough and wriggle beneath him. "I'm sick unto death of your bragging!"

But Richard's eyes flashed fury, and he grunted, "I do not brag! I tell what I've learned, and I alone! Maybe Smith saw I was the better choice of the two!"

"Not true!" said Nat. Richard bucked hard and rolled

over, throwing Nat off. He tried to jump to his feet, but Nat grabbed his leg and jerked it out from under him, toppling him. Nat hopped to his feet and kicked at Richard, but Richard was up again, throwing wild blows with his fist in the direction of Nat's face. Most missed; several smacked his jaw soundly, bringing on a star-rush of pain.

"You do not even know how to fight!" Nat tried to laugh. "You are truly a child, Richard, and don't even know how to act a man!"

Richard rushed Nat and fell into him. The two took the air for a moment, then struck the ground, knocking the breath from Nat's lungs and a grunt from Richard's lips. The arm Nat had hurt in the hold of the ship was cut through with a new shard of pain.

And suddenly Nat was being kicked soundly in the side, and it wasn't Richard, for Richard was prone beside him, pounding him with his hands and panting.

"Stupid dogs!" came a voice from above, accompanied by more painful kicks to the ribs. "Stop that fighting before I throw you both into the river for the fish to eat!"

Nat rolled away from the boot and stood, his head swimming and his stomach threatening to pitch its contents. Richard received a few more kicks to his hip before he was able to get up. The disciplinarian was Edward Pising, clearly in no mood for boys.

"You're more trouble than you're worth!" the man swore, waving the hatchet he held in his sweaty hand. "If I see this again, I'll knock your heads off, don't think I won't!"

Nat snatched up his axe, trying to ignore the ache in his side and the fresh agony in his arm, and went back to stripping bark. Richard did the same. Neither spoke.

The morning wore on. Men stopped from their jobs

of chopping, digging, and hammering to eat a meal of clams, berries, and leftover beef and hardtack from the ships. Gentlemen, who had occupied themselves with ordering the laborers about and complaining about everything from the smell of their tents to the lack of gold lying about on the top of the ground, sat by their fires and adjusted their collars and dabbed their sweaty foreheads with their handkerchiefs. The council president, Captain Wingfield, sat with Gabriel Archer, John Ratcliffe, and several of the gentlemen. Wingfield seemed to think gentlemen were right in keeping their hands clean. He seemed as lazy as the worst of them.

I should not want to be a man such as Wingfield, Nat thought. *He is even worse than the blubbering Edward Brookes. Brookes was not a very bright man, and in that is his excuse. But Wingfield is clearly shrewd. Yet look at him, dallying around as if the rest of us were servants.*

When no one was watching, Nat took a helmet, musket, and powder horn from the store tent and sneaked into the woods by the clearing. He knew it was dangerous and that the council would not approve, but he had to get away for a little while. Until Smith invited him on an expedition, he could at least check out the woods near the settlement.

He walked through the pines, as thick and as close together as old women telling each other secrets. He held the musket shoulder height. The underbrush was dense. Thorns grabbed his ankles, biting through the cotton stockings and into his flesh. Briars wrapped his sleeves and ripped them. But he kept on walking. He followed a winding stream a short ways, then climbed a boulder, slick with moss. He watched carefully, remembering the details of the landscape. When he had the chance, he would draw a map and keep it with his journal pages. This way he could return when the chance arose and find his riches alone.

The shadows in the woods were deep. Sunlight was swallowed up in the throats of the trees. Birds screamed overhead, mocking the young Englishman as he stumbled ahead. A vine wrapped around his bad foot and with a grunt he fell on his face, the musket flying from his grasp. His head struck a log, making a gash in his cheek and throwing stars in his field of vision.

"Ow," Nat moaned, rolling over onto his back and touching his face. Above him was the tangle of branches. Beneath him, the ground was slick and damp with mosses and lichens. Cautiously he rolled to his side.

"I'm doing poorly as an explorer," Nat sputtered, then took a long, deep breath. "Good thing Smith can't see me now. Brawling and tripping! Pitiful! Enough, now. Act as an explorer and you will be an explorer."

He looked straight ahead.

Staring at him from the brush was a pair of eyes.

Screaming, Nat sat bolt upright. His hands went out before him to protect himself. And then something came down firmly on his shoulder.

He screamed again.

A voice said, "What is the matter with you, Nat?"

Nat's head snapped around. Jehu Robinson stood there, one hand on Nat's shoulder, the other on the hilt of his sword.

"I saw eyes!" Nat said, panting. "There, look! Savages staring at me, ready to cut me to pieces!"

Nat and Jehu looked into the brush.

A strange animal, short, squatty, and fat, winked at them with a wet, confused gaze. The animal seemed to be wearing a black mask and its tail was encircled with rings. Its nose twitched, and it lumbered off beneath the low branches of a pine tree and out of sight.

"Savages?" asked Jehu. He stood up and chuckled.

"If that is the savage we expect to find near James Towne, then I would fear very little for our safety!"

Nat put his hand to his forehead. His legs hurt, his arm ached, his bad foot throbbed, and his face burned. And now embarrassment was heaped on top of it all. *I look like a fool!*

"Can you walk, Nat?"

Nat nodded. He wouldn't make things worse by letting on how bad he felt.

"Good, then. Come back with me to the site. John Smith is looking for you and I told him I knew where you were. I saw you go into the woods."

"Smith is looking for me?"

"Yes."

Why? Maybe Samuel's sick and he needs another page for a while. Maybe Smith's tent has torn and needed stitching. Surely it's nothing more than a menial task.

But maybe it is something important.

Nat snatched up the musket and followed Jehu back to the clearing. His heart beat heavily with expectation and he forgot how hurt he was. He glanced once over his shoulder and thought he saw eyes again, watching him intently from behind a tree trunk. But then Nat blinked and the eyes were gone.

Men were finished with the midday meal and were back at work. The steady thumping and cracking of axe and hatchet filled the air. Gentlemen paced about, sipping from their mugs, dabbing their noses, avoiding the suggestions by the council that they try their hand at digging for shellfish along the riverbank or shaving bark from the trees.

But what caught Nat's eye immediately was the shallop. It was back in the water again, and a number of men were inside, dressed in helmets and armor, grasping oars, readying to set off on another exploration.

Several bundles of provisions were in the boat. Smith stood by the shallop, talking to one of the soldiers and pointing up the river. Nat hurried over.

"Ah," said Smith, turning to Nat. "I need you to come on this trip. Bring your cloak and get into the shallop. Keep that helmet and musket and take up armor. We leave in just a moment."

Nat hurried to where he'd left his cloak hanging on a prickly branch of a pine tree. Richard was still slinging his axe, but he stopped when he saw Nat.

"I've been chosen," Nat said.

Richard wiped his face. "Chosen for what?"

"To go on an expedition up the river with John Smith!"

Richard threw down the axe. "You? They asked for you to go instead of me? But I've already proven myself! Where are they going?"

"Does it matter? An adventure. Now I must go. They are nearly ready to leave."

Richard grabbed his axe and slammed it into the wood with so much force that a huge shower of splinters rose into the air like a swarm of locusts.

Nat couldn't help but grin. Richard was such a child sometimes. But down at the shallop, as Nat put his musket inside, Smith said, "Oh, please ask the Mutton boy to come, too. I need him on this trip."

Nat's grin fell. He walked halfway back to Richard, waved at him, and jerked his thumb in the direction of the shallop. Richard understood. With a whoop and cheer, he ran for his gear and joined the others by the river.

The shallop was pushed into the water, everyone took a paddle, and they headed northwest.

❧ 10 ❧

May 19, 1607

THE SHALLOP WAS more comfortable than the pinnace, although it was in no way a luxury ship. There was a bit more room, and with so many men rowing, twelve on each side, none had the full brunt of the task. Nat sat near the back between two men he did not know. He didn't talk to anyone, but followed the others' lead in dipping, pulling, and lifting the oar through the river's bright water.

Richard was near the front of the boat next to Smith, and he was rowing, too, although he could barely keep up.

Why did Smith want him along? Nat wondered. *He surely is no help at all.*

In the humidity off the river, Nat's face, arms, and back were quickly covered in a slick sheen of sweat, and his arms grew tired with the motions. But he would die before he let the men know this. He was acting a sailor.

He felt good. He felt free.

Men near the back of the shallop gossiped about the precious metals they hoped to find on this particular trip, while in the front, Smith directed loudly, boasting that it would not be long before he helped them discover a short passage to the Pacific Ocean and secured himself yet more fame in the eyes of all English sailors and the king himself. "We find ourselves far remote from men and means," said Smith. "Yet it is here that we shall discover the glory of a new route and bring England's power beyond that ever known on earth! All other countries henceforth shall be cowed by the mere mention of England's name and shall keep away for fear of our immutable power."

There was murmured agreement, and Nat found his smile widening in spite of the growing weariness of his arms. Virginia was truly the place of opportunity for all.

They had been gone just over an hour upriver when Smith directed the shallop into a smaller tributary. This they followed until the creek became too shallow and reed-infested to venture farther. They would have to go back and travel farther upriver. Everyone climbed from the shallop and stood hip-deep as the shallop was turned around.

And then an arrow smacked into the shallop, nailing a sailor's forearm to the wood. He shrieked. Men spun about in the stream, trying to shoulder muskets and prepare for a fight, but it was too late. On the bank was a gathering of natives, bows drawn and arrows pointed at the Englishmen.

There was a very long moment of silence and staring. The only sounds were that of the water coursing around the men and the shallop, the birds nearby, and the heavy breathing of the man whose arm was pinned to the wood.

Richard, up to his neck in the murky water, lost his balance, cried out, slipped, and went underwater. Smith grabbed him up and shook him, growling that he should hold still and wait quietly.

Another long minute passed as the men in the water and the natives on the shore studied each other. The natives were nearly naked, wearing only leather or grass loincloths. Their hair was shaved on the right side; the left was very long and coated with some sort of oil. Some of the men had this hair twisted into a knot with birds' wings and pieces of antler woven through. One man's hair even appeared to have a dried human hand laced in it.

Nat felt his bladder go loose with fear; and it was only with a very small sense of relief that he was standing deep in the water.

Suddenly one native jumped into the water as the others stood motionless, the bows and arrows still trained at the Englishmen. The native reached the pinned sailor, wrapped his hands about the arrow, and jerked it free. The sailor made no sound other than a horrific grunting through his teeth, and he drew the bloodied arm up to his chest.

Now that the natives had made a move, Smith seemed confident to do the same. He raised one hand, palm flat, and dipped his head in a small movement of greeting. Nat sensed the gesture was to mean peace, although with the wounding of the sailor, Nat found it hard to believe Smith could offer anything on peaceful terms. But Smith was a survivor, and Nat had no choice but to follow his lead.

Several soldiers and sailors made the same gestures that Smith had. The natives conferred quietly among each other, and then one whirled his hand to welcome the settlers onto the bank of the creek.

Slowly, eying each other cautiously and the natives even more so, the men pulled themselves from the creek and followed the natives into the woods.

Two young natives, about Nat's age, brought up the

rear, slapping their bows in the brush and talking softly.

Nat and Richard were near the back of the group, keeping as close to the other men as possible without running into them.

"They are going to kill us," Richard murmured. "How could Smith have let us go with them this way? Should we have not fought with our muskets?"

"Be quiet," Nat said, although he was certain the terrified pounding of his heart could be heard as surely as the pounding of English boot-steps on the ground.

They came to a clearing, and in it, a tiny village. About fifteen houses sat about in no sense of pattern and with no true lanes. These houses were small with rounded roofs and covered with mats of marsh reeds. In one spot there was a grove of fruit trees, and in another place a variety of crops were growing. A tiny, three-sided hut on stilts was in the center of the garden, and a boy holding a long branch peeked out and stared at the strangers. Small boys in loincloths and small girls with no clothes at all came out from the houses and watched, wide-eyed, as the Englishmen were led through the village. Adults then joined them, men and women, who knelt on the ground and dug at the dirt with their nails and made loud noises.

Let those be sounds of joy and not of vengeance! Nat prayed.

They came then to a cabin much longer than the others, and covered with bark instead of the reed mats. Smith, who had regained a straight, confident stride and smile, went into the longhouse with three of the natives while the rest stayed outside and worked at maintaining their composure. The wounded man had torn a strip of his white sleeve and wrapped the arm up. The citizens of the town gathered near, speaking with the native warriors who had brought the men to the village. There was laughter and dramatic waving of hands in describing the encounter. Nat watched them out of the corner of his eye, trying not to seem concerned or afraid, but trying desperately to figure out what they were conveying to each other.

"Are they going to torture us?" Richard whispered.

"Hush!" said Nat. He tried again to decipher the natives' words and motions. It was worthless. The language and the gestures were agonizingly alien.

After nearly twenty minutes, John Smith came back out of the house, led by the natives who had gone in with him. And then came another native, dressed in a mantle of such feathered, pearled, and shelled finery that Nat knew he was a leader. He held his head high, and his eyes were narrowed in an expression of superiority. All the other villagers showed respect for him by stepping back and not looking him in the eye.

They were taken next to a place near the center of the village where woven mats had been placed. The leader, who Smith explained quietly and briefly was the village *weroance*, lowered himself onto a mat at the head of the circle. Only then did everyone else sit. For the next half hour the Englishmen were entertained with strange dancing and singing. While a man beat on a leather instrument and sang, men and women alike took turns dancing before the *weroance* and the visitors. Feet stamped in rhythm with the drumming. Natives in the circle clapped along. The singing was bizarre and hypnotic.

Then food was served, a wide array of cooked fish, beans, berries, fruits, and a bland gruel. Nat, sitting crossed-legged as everyone else, tried to eat, although his stomach would have none of it. It clamped and clenched, trying to throw the morsels back into his mouth along with stinging bile. With great effort he forced the food down. After that, he only pretended to eat. Although the air was cool, sweat beaded on his arms and neck, and he swiped at it anxiously. Next to him, Richard seemed to have as much trouble partaking of the food as Nat.

At last the dancing and music stopped, and the *weroance* stretched and stood. The shells on his mantle clicked heavily. John Smith waited until the *weroance* nodded, and then he, too, stood. He went over and gestured to the *weroance*. None of it made sense to Nat. The *weroance* tilted his head as if considering, then swept his hand out toward the nearest field of crops.

And then Smith pointed at Richard.

Richard gasped.

Nat's heart froze. The fish he had been holding between his teeth was coughed out involuntarily. He spit it into his hand and then wiped it into the dust.

Why is he pointing at Richard?

"Mutton," Smith called. "Come over here to me."

The Englishmen looked at Richard. Several seemed as confused as he, but others nodded solemnly in understanding.

"Richard Mutton, come here!"

Richard stood shakily and walked over to John Smith. Was Smith going to introduce Richard to the leader as a gesture of friendship? Was Smith so proud of Richard that he wanted to point him out to the leader? Or, perhaps, had the *weroance*, who had begun to study Richard's pale blond hair with his fingers, decided Richard was some kind of strange creature?

Smith put his hand on Richard's shoulder. Richard looked at the ground.

What is going on? Nat wondered.

Smith said, "You will stay here, Richard. You have been traded for goodwill and for baskets of food these savages will give us to take back to James Towne."

Nat's mouth dropped open. He stared at Smith in

utter disbelief. Fear had sucked more color from Richard's face than seasickness ever had.

"Men," Smith said to his soldiers and sailors. "Come with me, and we will be given all we can carry on our shallop. Baskets of all the good things we feasted on this day. It will help keep our settlement alive until our own crops come in good and strong."

Then Richard grabbed at Smith's sleeve. "Wait! What is this you are doing to me? Have you lost your mind, sir?"

Smith laughed. "Some would say I lost it long ago. Now sit, Richard. These natives will not harm you if you are not obstinate. You are but a boy. Do you really think I brought you to Virginia as a laborer? You are much too small. Be silent and the natives will not find you a threat." He strode off to join his men, but Richard ran, too, and stopped just in front of the captain. He grabbed Smith's sleeve.

"You cannot leave me, sir! I cannot survive here in this place!"

Smith clenched his jaw. "Get back before I knock you back!"

"Don't leave me!"

"This is the way of explorers, trading boys for food or goodwill," said Smith. "It has always been so."

"Please!" Richard's voice cracked and spun into sobs. "I do not know what to do. How should I act, sir?"

Nat's stomach twisted.

A soldier said, "Push the boy aside, Captain. These savages will have little to do with such demonstrations as that boy is having." The soldier grabbed Richard by the neck and shoved him backward. Smith led the men away. Nat trailed, afraid to look back over his shoulder. Afraid of what he would see in the eyes of the natives and in the eyes of the boy who had made this long, difficult journey with him from London.

"Nat, don't leave me!" he heard Richard cry.

"I have no choice!" Nat said to himself.

And he didn't turn around. The sound of taunting, laughing village children made the hair on his arms stand up. But he marched on.

11

May 24, 1607

We are back at the fort at James Towne. I am again assigned to strip tree bark and to help set the planks in the ground to secure the walls.

But my heart is sick. It is all I can do to keep my mind from the terror I saw in Richard's eyes when we left him behind with those savages. What is happening to him now? What is his fate? And the last words between us were angry. It is too late to take them back, but they haunt me.

Nicholas Skot and Samuel Collier have become skittish. They work at dragging wood from forest to fort but, like Richard, neither is a large boy. I told them what happened to Richard, and they wonder if they will be the next to be traded if there is a need. Back on the ship I would have enjoyed the fear I see in Samuel's eyes, but now it is only a reminder of Richard's fate. Nicholas has told me he will run to the woods before being taken like a sheep to slaughter at the hands of John Smith.

Smith. I know the captain is brave and strong and does what he deems right, but I know now that I do not want to be a man like Smith.

And so when my mind has a moment of rest from thoughts of Richard I wonder—whom should I imitate? Where is a man I can act like? Where is a man I can become?

12

June 9, 1607

Three days ago, as John Smith was out again exploring, we at the James Towne fort were attacked by natives. Such a frightful howl we heard as we stood with our axes and awls, bringing down yet more trees to be split and hauled to the place of construction. We dropped our tools and took up our muskets. Many hadn't time to load the powder and shot before a rain of arrows came down on us. Men dropped like stones, wounded in shoulder and leg and chest. But I was able to fire as the natives came into sight at the edge of the clearing, hitting one native in the throat. He dropped his bow and his knees buckled. His eyes glared at me as he fell dead to the ground. I only remember one other man with such hate and fear in his eyes, and that was a convicted traitor in London as he was taken away on a wagon to be drawn and quartered.

Two hundred warriors there were, according to Edward Wingfield. More than all of us together. Yet the roar of our muskets scared them off and we were left to tend our injured men.

I asked Edward Pising why we would be attacked. As many others, I had thought we had established goodwill. But Pising said he did not know. Perhaps this was another village whom we had not appeased. *Perhaps we had done something offensive which the savages had witnessed while peering at us from the forest.*

"Who can know their minds? Surely not us," he said. "And this shows we can in no way trust them as Smith is bound to think at times."

Now, with some bandaged and others healing in their tents, we work faster than before. We must get our fort constructed.

13

August 19, 1607

"THE CROPS WE'VE raised are deplorable," said Jehu as he and Nat jammed their shovels into the soil within the palisade walls of James Towne fort. The man's black hair was stringy and his eyes pinched with worry. He had also lost a great deal of weight since May, as had all the other settlers. "What seed we brought from England was half moldy when we put it into the ground. We'll be lucky if we see any fall vegetables or wheat at all."

"How do you know so much?" Nat asked. "You are a shareholder who has come to Virginia to find gold. Gentlemen don't know about crops and digging."

Jehu tossed a shovelful of soil out onto the nearby pile. He and Nat were digging a new well. The first one had not provided enough water for the settlement. This second one would hopefully give enough fresh water for the men and animals and crops alike. The water in the James River was brackish, laced with salt and grit. Some men, in moments of desperate thirst, had drunk of the river and found themselves seriously ill or dead.

"I was not always a gentleman," said Jehu. "My fortune came from good planning and a little bit of luck. My parents were farmers from Scotland, but I learned merchanting when I went to live with my uncle in London at fourteen. I have been successful and lucky. Yes, I want gold. But I want to survive to enjoy the riches, and that will take the efforts of us all."

Nat nodded, and slammed his shovel into the growing hole of the well.

The Virginia summer sun above was barely tolerable. No longer were breezes fresh and the air agreeable as they had been in May. Days and nights alike were hot and oppressive. Insects sucked blood of the men, leaving many unwell. Some had died from the bites of these insects; other had perished from eating spoiled food left from the voyage and drinking the river water. A total of twenty-seven men were dead. Even Bartholomew Gosnold, the captain of the *Godspeed*, was so ill with an intestinal disorder many doubted he would recover.

Food was growing scarce; the men had eaten adequately the first weeks, dining on the remaining victuals brought from England. Now deer and squirrels were killed by those who could hunt, and the river gave up fish, turtles, and crabs to those who could gather them, but there was not enough to feed everyone. The garden outside the James Towne fortress was tended regularly, commoners and laborers hoeing, watering, and keeping away as many scavenging animals and burrowing insects as possible. But the crops that had come up were meager. Beans were tiny and few; peas were the same. Cabbages and squash were riddled with an unknown blight. The wheat crop was scrawny. Come autumn, life would be harder still, with little food in store.

If the gentlemen would learn to hunt and garden like com-

moners, Nat had written in his journal two nights prior, *then there might be enough food. But they are worthless. They complain and eat, no better than leeches. There is even talk that our council president Edward Maria Wingfield has been pilfering food from the storehouse to feed himself and his friends. I believe it may be true, as he seems less thin than the rest of us. Lazy, selfish man! But how long can the storehouse feed him before there is nothing left? He will have a hard lesson once his own belly screams at him. Indeed, all these gentlemen have hard lessons to learn if they are to survive more than this summer!*

It is best for me to watch out for myself, for if I depend on others, I shall surely starve.

Jehu and Nat worked another few hours on the well, then took a break. Nat put his helmet on his head and picked up his shirt and musket. He went out through the fort's gate, along one of the grassy pathways, past the fenced gardens and down to the river's edge. He sat on a favorite stone and slipped his shirt on. The fabric made him sweat more, but at least it kept most of the biting flies off his skin. Gazing out across the wide stretch of water, Nat thought about many things. As always, Richard came to mind first.

I wonder if he is alive. Perhaps he is truly safe. I'll never know. There was nothing I could do. If I'd come to Richard's aid, what might have happened to me? As I had to be silent when at John Smith's court of inquiry, I had to be silent at Richard's trading.

Natives, whom Smith called Powhatans after the name of the chief Powhatan of all the native villages in the near and far reaches of this land, had attacked off and on through the summer, but no attack was as severe as the one in June. This had encouraged the men to hasten the completion of the fort. The soldiers set cannons atop bulwarks at the corners of the fort. The Powhatans were, it seemed, a warring group of people with minds impossible for Nat to understand. They appeared friendly at times, then bloodthirsty at others.

Smith had at last gained his seat on the council because of his ability to deal with the unpredictable Powhatans. If it weren't for him, Nat was certain that the whole settlement would be dead or enslaved by now. But Nat no longer trusted Smith on a personal level.

Nat had fared better than most men since May. He covered himself with river mud at times to keep mosquitoes and biting flies away, he slept lightly to listen for impending attacks, and he always hid away in his sack a portion of biscuit or dried meat from each meal so that when cold weather came, he would have something to keep going. As of now, he had many handfuls of salt beef and pork, some dried apples, and a number of rock-hard biscuits. Most of it was wormy, but Nat had pulled the worms out. It was not the first time he'd hoarded food. In London he could go days without finding a fresh supply, and keeping a bit aside was a wise boy's actions. If the other members of James Towne were smart, they would be doing the same.

Some of the buildings in James Towne were already complete, including the church, the storehouse, and cottages for the council members and some gentlemen. The structures were tedious to build, made of woven willow and hazel branches and plastered with thick mud and covered with thatched roofs.

But many men still slept in the rotting tents. Nat shared a tent with Samuel Collier, a young tailor named William Love, and an older laborer named John Laydon. Neither Love nor Laydon was a big talker, and the animosity between Nat and Samuel remained strong. This was good; Nat didn't have to endure late-night banter from any of them.

"There is a gold-seeking party leaving in the morning. Are you going?"

Nat looked around. Jehu was there, standing behind the stone on which Nat sat, slipping his own shirt on over his broad shoulders and scanning the river with squinting eyes.

"Gold? Now?" said Nat. "Those men are fools. Will gold feed them or protect them from attack? I think not. Gold is in my future, not my present."

"Wise," said Jehu. He sat on the rock beside Nat, picked up a stray; flat pebble, and flung it toward the water. It skipped four times and disappeared. "Can you do more than four?"

Nat took a flat stone and hurled it. It skipped three times before it went under.

"I've been thinking. There are many plants here in Virginia," said Jehu. "Different from those in England, but some of which are edible, I'm certain. If only we had a way of finding out which we can eat and which are poisonous. We could then gather the good plants and dry them to add to our store for the coming winter."

"We could ask the Powhatans," Nat said sourly.

"We could," said Jehu. "But the more we can discover ourselves, the better. We don't want to seem helpless to the natives, although I think they already see us as such. I have heard your belly growl, Nathaniel. Don't tell me you aren't hungry and that you don't want to ease that pain."

"I hear my belly, but I don't feel it. I've been hungry much of my life. London was a harsh mother. Hunger is so familiar I scarcely notice."

"Ah, but you will. Give it time."

Nat threw another stone into the water. It skipped twice and sank. "Are you proposing we choose a committee to taste plants? Those that kill the men we will not eat and those the men survive we will harvest?"

"A committee, no," said Jehu. "But volunteers might take small tastes."

"There will never be such volunteers," Nat said.

"I will volunteer. A small taste of a dangerous plant will likely only make one sick. Will you join me? If we discover new foods, what a great thing that will be. We can be of service to all the men here."

"No," said Nat.

Jehu nodded slowly. "I understand," he said. He patted Nat on the shoulder and went back to the fort.

"He will only get himself killed," Nat said to himself. "If not an arrow or bad water or an insect bite, he will intentionally poison himself. Idiot."

Nat went back to the fort when Reverend Hunt rang the bell for the daily worship in the church, and Jehu didn't mention his plan again.

❧ 14 ❧

September 4, 1607

I've a little time to write. This ink and paper is from the bratty page's sack of goods. I sit in my smelly tent, but neither Samuel Collier nor John Laydon nor William Love, the three who share this tent with me, is here at the moment.

More than fifty of our men are dead now, with Captain Gosnold one of the number. Some men have been killed by the illnesses and starvation, others by arrows, and still another recently executed for treason against the crown. He dared to jump up during our worship service and shout that the king was a tyrant who cared nothing about us here in James Towne. Soldiers took him and dragged him out of the church and on the spot, without inquiry or comment, shot him under the order of the council. Poor fool! This action seemed to me more savage than savages, for surely the man was mad with fear and hunger.

The Susan Constant and Godspeed, which left with Captain Newport in June, will be gone until early winter, most likely. No new supplies can be counted on until then.

Many men seem to think we have been abandoned, like the colony that was begun on Roanoke Island south of here years ago. They were left alone and when someone at last came from

*England to see the progress and bring more settlers, they dis-
covered that the entire colony was gone. Everyone had disappeared. Taken away or killed by natives is the guess. Is that
what will happen to us?*

*If Richard is alive, is he perhaps better off with natives than
with incompetent Englishmen? I miss having someone to complain to about Samuel and Archer and the whining gentlemen.*

*This afternoon, while I was clearing thistled brush from the
edge of the forest, I again spied a pair of eyes glaring at me
from behind a boulder. Another animal, I thought, but this
time a large one. I held still in case it was a bear, making no
sound. No one working near me had any idea that there was
danger so close, within several feet.*

*I continued to stare at the eyes. Then they shifted and wid-
ened, and I knew the eyes to be human and not animal. I felt
a shout rattle my throat, but it did not come out. A Powhatan,
so close he could have slit my throat as I bent to chop the
brush. I prayed God that I would not be murdered where I
stood.*

*"You pause there! Peacock, get back to work!" Captain Ar-
cher shouted to me. The man, who would never so much as
lift an axe, had come out with those of us who would, and
he was standing, throwing his hands all over and shaking
his head madly, like a crazed fishwife.*

*I didn't know what else to do, with the Powhatan watching
me. And so I did what I most often do, I began to act. When
Archer looked elsewhere, I imitated him silently, throwing my
own arms around, tossing my head back and forth and wag-
ging my tongue.*

*The Powhatan began to laugh. I saw the bushes shake and
I heard a high chuckle. Such a strange, soft sound! I had no
idea a native could laugh. He parted the brush with his hands
and smiled at me. It was a boy, a bit younger than myself,
wearing bear grease and a leather cloth, his black hair una-*

dorned and slicked back. He pointed at me as if he liked the joke, then let go of the brush and vanished.

I remind myself daily that I will become what I'd imagined back in London. An adventurer, a wealthy, independent man. I know how to plant crops now, and I have learned to cut and strip wood. It is a start. Gold may have to wait until next year. But I will have it.

Jehu continues his lone search for edible plants. I have told him I cannot feel hunger. That was a lie, but I will never show my discomfort. Jehu has discovered some berries which are quite good and dry quite well. He has found a tuber which is tough but meaty. As of now, he has only been mildly sick with a wild bean he tasted. God watches over fools, it seems. Maybe God will watch over James Towne.

❧ 15 ❧

September 7, 1607

"Do that again, young Peacock," said John Laydon as he sat down on a tree stump with a tin plate of wheat gruel in his lap. The food was tasteless and watery, made of remaining grain from the bottom of the barrels brought on the ships in May and some tiny beans from the James Towne garden. Soon there would be no food at all except what the men produced themselves. Yet many gentlemen still refused to work. John Smith insisted that the council force everyone to work, but Wingfield, Archer, and Kendall would have nothing of it. They didn't want to make enemies of the gentlemen. At the moment, everyone, including the gentlemen, was seated within and without the fortress, eating the slimy gruel.

Nat was seated on the ground. His shirt was off and he could see his ribs straining at the skin of his chest. "Do what again?"

John Laydon leaned over and with a tired smirk said, "The imitation of Archer. I saw you the other day when we were cutting trees. You performed a hilarious rendition of the captain. I told several friends and they want to see it."

Nat noticed that a couple of other men had turned and were grinning at him. Was Laydon serious?

Laydon said, "Archer is not nearby. Please. We need something to laugh at."

The other men nodded.

Nat checked to make sure that no one else was looking his way, stood and went through the motions. He shook his head, snarled, jabbed his finger at Laydon, and jammed his hand on his hip, as he'd seen Archer do many times. John Laydon and the other men clutched their bony sides and howled with laughter.

"Good show!" said Laydon.

Nat sat and licked the remaining gruel from the plate.

In the days that followed, word spread around James Towne that Nat was a comedian. He was stopped as he drew water from the well, while knee-deep in the river digging for mussels, and even as he tried to sneak away to walk in the woods.

"Psst," said one soldier standing on the bulwark. "Peacock, show me an imitation of our council president, the dreaded Edward Maria Wingfield."

Nat wrinkled his nose and made his lip twitch. Then he stomped his foot and leaned back, pretending to down a mug of the beer Wingfield enjoyed so much, then staggered as if intoxicated. The soldier chuckled heartily.

"Hey, there, boy," said the gentleman Benjamin Beast as Nat passed Beast's cottage late one evening on the way to his own tent. "Come in, I've something for you to do." Nat went inside the cottage, which was dark and stank of diarrhea and vomit. There, another gentleman named George Walker was sick, rolled up in a blanket and shivering.

"My friend is ill. I want you to cheer him," said Beast. "We understand you have a talent for satire. Please perform as Captain Smith, that crooked, impudent old arse!"

So Nat pretended to be Smith the way the gentlemen saw the man. He tossed back an invisible cape, tugged at a neck ruff, and crossed his eyes as if on the verge of insanity. Then he went into a mock battle with invisible Turks, cutting off heads and bowing. Beast and George Walker chortled and nodded, then gave Nat his leave. Beast pressed a bruised half apple into Nat's hand as a thank-you.

Back in his tent, Nat lay down on his straw mattress near the dozing, whistle-nosed Samuel Collier, and took out pen and page. He wrote, *If entertaining keeps me in good graces with the men of James Towne, so be it. I will not always have to perform at their beck and call. But for now, if they want a drunken councilor, I'll give them one. If they want a lazy sailor, they can have him. If they ask for a constipated gentleman, thus I shall be.*

❧ 16 ❧

September 12, 1607

"WHAT IS WRONG with your face, boy? It is covered with maggots! Let me get them off before they eat your eyes!"

Nat dropped his hoe and straightened from his work in the wheat garden, beads of sweat rolling down his face. Before him, standing unsteadily with a sword in trembling hands, was Jehu Robinson. Two other gardeners stopped their work and stared.

"He's gone mad," one man hissed.

"Nathaniel Peacock," said Jehu. His words were slurred. "You've got worms all over your head. Hold still while I chop them away!"

Jehu wrapped his fingers around the handle of the sword, and with a grunt, swung it up and over. It arced by Nat's ear and Nat jumped out of the way, swearing.

"Jehu! What have you eaten? You are delirious!"

"Nat, wait!" said Jehu. "The worms are in your nostrils now. You will smother to death!" He lifted his sword and lashed out at Nat again. Nat again darted out of the way.

"Jehu, drop the sword!"

The two men in the garden ran out of the gate and up toward the fort, calling for help. "We've a madman!"

Jehu continued to wield the sword, Nat continued to dodge him. The man's awkward movements made it easy to keep away from the blow of the deadly blade. "Please, Jehu," said Nat. "What have you eaten that has you so crazed?"

Jehu paused for a moment, then pulled several leaves from his pocket. They were ordinary-looking, with thorny stems. "These taste peculiar," Jehu said. His eyes went shut, and then opened again, filmy and senseless. He dropped the leaves.

"Put down the sword," Nat said. "Please."

"But the worms . . . !"

"There are no worms, man, listen to me!"

There was whooping and shouting now at the fort. Nat looked up and saw three soldiers rushing down to the wheat garden, muskets at the ready.

"Drop your weapon, Jehu!" said Nat.

Jehu spun around on his toe and saw the soldiers racing at him. He shivered violently and raised the sword. "Devils!" he screamed. "You've devils in your midst!"

"Jehu," said Nat. "There are no devils. Lower the sword."

"Don't you see them?" shrieked Jehu. "God help me, they are sharp-toothed devils, come to slay me!"

"No!" said Nat.

Jehu charged forward, out of the garden and up the ridge toward the men, brandishing his sword. There was a moment of silence as the men paused to aim the muskets and then there was an explosion as three muskets fired. One musket ball struck Jehu in his right shoulder, shattering it instantly and making him drop the sword. The other hit his right knee, and he collapsed with a wail on to the ground. The third lodged in the man's gut, and his shirt flowered with a bright red blossom of blood.

The men with the muskets came over cautiously and poked at Jehu with their shoes.

"He's dead," said one.

"Brain fever of some sort," said a third man. "He's best off dead than a danger to himself and the rest of us."

But he might have recovered, Nat thought. *If they had only disarmed him and put him in a cottage, he might have come through this in just a little while!*

"You, boy," said one man to Nat. "Help take this man into the fort. We'll give him a proper burial."

Nat wanted to cry out at these men, to scold them for their haste, for now dead was a man who had no other thought over the past months than how he could help the settlement survive. But Nat could not cry out. He would not bring their wrath down on himself.

Nat took Jehu's arms and a soldier took his legs. They proceeded into the fortress, where he was laid in the chapel and Reverend Hunt bid all to attend a funeral service. The men gathered solemnly, helmets in hands, listening as the minister spoke of Jehu's generosity and wisdom.

Nat stood near the back beside the open doorway, between Nicholas Skot and Samuel Collier. Nicholas was clearly upset, and wiped his eyes with his hands as the reverend spoke. Samuel, for all his ingrained haughtiness, seemed distracted and dazed, staring down at his shoe tips and rolling his lips in and out between his teeth. It was hard to breathe inside the church, even though the building was not as crowded as it had been months ago with so many men dead. Nat's chest ached in what was more than just heat exhaustion. Something harsh and stinging pressed behind his eyes. He thought not only of Jehu, but of Richard—poor Richard, vanished among the Powhatans and never heard from again—and of his dead mother and of the dead boy James Brumfield, killed on the shore of Cape Henry, and of the dead boys he had once thieved with back in England.

If you cry, they will never again see you the way you want them to. You dare not cry, not now, not ever!

Nat clenched one fist in the other, and bit the inside of his cheek until it bled. But the tears did not come.

Jehu was buried within the fort. Then everyone went back to their normal routines, the gentlemen preparing for the next gold search, the councilors making sure laborers wasted no time on the construction of more cottages within the fortress, the soldiers manning the cannons which faced the forest, and the others wearily raking the river bottom with wood rakes for clams and crabs and chasing animals from the gardens and grumbling that they wished they had the hunting skills of the cursed natives.

After Jehu's burial, Nat paced the fortress. He walked back and forth from the church, past the tents and cottages and storehouse to the gate and back again. From within some of the cottages he could hear the moans of those who were ill with fever and starvation. His nerves clawed the inside of his skin.

"Jehu, you moron," he said to himself. "I told you not to try plants you didn't know!"

He picked up several stones and hurled them through the fence of the sheep's pen. It struck a ewe and her lamb, who squeaked and took several sideways, stumbling steps.

Then Nat stopped in front of Captain Smith's cottage. Smith was not there. Nat glanced around, then went inside.

The captain's home was neat. His wood and canvas cot had a wool blanket neatly folded at the end. On a wooden stool were writing utensils and a comb and knife. Several small crates were beneath the cot. Clothes, an extra shirt and vest and pairs of stockings, hung on nails driven into the wood framing.

Nat stooped down and pulled the crates from beneath the cot. He opened the first. In it were books and scrolls. Nat shut it and opened a second. Here were even more clothes, smelling of mildew, and an extra pair of shoes. Nat slammed it, too.

The third crate, smallest of them all, had a lock. Nat stood and kicked the lock solidly with the bottom of his shoe. The lock didn't break, but the lid of the crate cracked and Nat tossed the lock aside. He opened the box.

"Ah," he said in a whisper.

Here were trinkets, the ones Smith used when coaxing the Powhatans into peace or food. There were small looking glasses and bits of smoothed metal and patches of silk fabric stitched into pouches with drawstrings. At the bottom, blue glass beads. They were smooth and cool. These seemed to be the most popular trade item. Back in July, three entire deer were given to James Towne in exchange for a single bead, which the *weroance* who had approved the gift immediately strung with deer sinew and put around his neck as a symbol of his status.

He scooped up six of the beads and shoved them into his pocket. They clacked softly against the pebbles from the bank of the Thames.

A spear of excitement jabbed Nat's gut as he collected a helmet and left the fort. It was like being in London again, snatching a fish from the monger's barrow. He was a good thief. It was a talent he'd not practiced in quite some time. Now he would bury the beads where no one would find them and accuse him of theft, which would surely bring a noose to his neck. In time he might be able to use these beads to trade for food for himself.

The forest was more dense than it had been in the spring, with summer growth holding tight, the leaves of the tall trees linked together overhead in a solid canopy and the vines growing lush below. Nat carefully avoided one particular vine with tri-leaves which the men had discovered gave a dreadfully itchy rash where it touched.

This part of the woods was familiar. Nat had walked here enough to know the rise and fall of the land. He had even sketched a simple map from his memory, and the map was safely stored in his sack with his journal pages. He felt nearly as home here among the trees as he did back at the fort, although he knew to always walk softly and listen well. He'd not seen any sign of gold, but that didn't mean it wasn't there. It was probably just below the soil, and soon he would take time to dig.

Then he found a good spot. It was close to the river, although the water was hard to see because of the undergrowth. The ground was mushy and covered with pine needles. Nat clawed soil up with his fingernails and tossed it aside. He reached into his pocket for the beads. He would put them here, cover them with soil and leaves, and mark the place with stones.

Suddenly something slammed into Nat's back and sent him flying through the air. He struck the ground on his shoulder with a grunt. Instantly Nat rolled onto his back and jumped to his feet. He would fight, he would survive!

Standing there with a look of triumph on his face was the Powhatan boy he'd seen from the garden. The boy had his hands out before him, one empty and one holding a writhing, copper-colored snake. Nat stared, his knees shaking.

The boy pointed at Nat, then the snake. He made a wriggling motion with his free hand, indicating that the snake had been traveling along the ground. Then he made a jabbing motion as if showing the snake had wanted to bite Nat on the ankle.

Nat slowly nodded at the boy. *Thank you.* The boy nodded back. *You are welcome.* The boy laughed. Nervously Nat laughed, too.

The boy whirled the struggling snake in the air and slapped it hard against a tree trunk. The snake went limp. The boy smiled and pointed at the snake and then to his mouth. Did the boy mean that the snake could be eaten? The boy held the snake out to Nat. Nat took it. He stared at it. Then he remembered how much the Powhatan boy had enjoyed the imitation of Gabriel Archer. Nat dropped the dead snake on the ground and then hunched over and pretended to sneak up on it. Then he quickly snatched it up and struggled with it as if it were still alive.

"Ah!" shouted the Powhatan, thrilled with the act. He began to slap at the dead snake, too. Both Nat and the boy laughed. Nat threw the snake against a tree, wiped his brow dramatically, and put the snake into his pocket. The head hung out limply.

"Ahhhh!" the boy repeated, smiling. The boy stared at Nat expectantly. Nat stared at the boy.

Laughing Boy, Nat thought. *It is what I will call him. But what does he want? He saved me from that serpent, surely. I suppose I should thank him for saving my life, but how do I do that?*

Nat thought of the rocks in his pocket. Maybe a smooth stone from London would be a good gift. Nat pulled out a quartz and gestured for the boy to take it.

The boy took the rock, turned it over, shook his head, and threw the rock to the ground.

Reluctantly Nat drew a glass bead from his pocket. The boy's eyes widened at this, and he took it with a whistle of admiration. He smiled at Nat, opened the leather pouch he wore tied to his waist, and dropped the bead inside. And then, as swiftly as before, he jumped off the path and was gone.

"He knows how to survive," Nat thought, pulling the snake half out of his pocket and then cramming it back again. "I bet I could learn a lot if I spent time with him. And I bet he would help me search for gold. I wonder if we'll meet again."

And the thought was funny, Nat realized as he finished burying the rest of the glass beads. For the first time he could remember, he was thinking that someone to help him might be all right. If only on occasion.

17

November 8, 1607

My excursions into the forests now often find me with a companion. Every ten days or so, as I work in the pitiful, dying gardens, harvesting the last of the crops and killing the late-season insects, I see familiar eyes by the boulder at the edge of the woods. It makes me glad, for I know I will have an adventure and will have some time away from the sickness and arguments of James Towne!

Laughing Boy has taught me how to hunt the way the Powhatans do. He showed me that two hunters can more easily kill a deer by chasing the animal into an inlet of the river, where it struggles in the soft river bottom and cannot get out. This makes it an easy target for musket or arrow. The first time, however, it was I who fell into the river bottom and struggled there, while Laughing Boy howled at me with joy and had a great moment at my expense. But we tried again and again, and it was not long before I was feeling agile and prepared.

Three times now I have come back to the fort with a deer, but not before Laughing Boy and I have made fires with tinder and sharpened stones and cooked and ate a portion of the animal. The men at James Towne were impressed that I, simple comedian that I am, was able to single-handedly hunt a deer. Of course, they demanded that I share. And so I handed the animal over, with a story that a bear had chased me with the carcass, and ripped part off.

"All three times a bear chased you?" Samuel Collier asked me with a sneer as John Laydon took the deer through the fortress gate. "Who could believe such a story from a boy who not months ago was begging for scraps from the doorsteps of the fishwives of London?"

"Yes," I told the little hot-bird in a whisper. "All three times. The bear thought the carcass was you."

Laughing Boy has also taught me to climb trees and patiently watch for small animals instead of scaring them away with the sound of my footsteps. I've had a hard time handling bow and arrow, but we amuse each other, making fun of my clumsy attempts which often send an arrow flying straight up in the air or smacking down into the ground. But five times now, I've brought back to James Towne several of the ringtailed creatures, but often as not, I hide one down the front of my shirt to cook and eat on my own at night.

I know I can survive Virginia! I shall outlive them all!

Several times I've tried to show Laughing Boy how to write. He likes to draw the animals he hunts and pictures of what I can only guess are his family. A father, three sisters, and a mother. A weroance.

No man at James Towne could possibly understand my trust of Laughing Boy. But no matter. I have to do what I have to do, and the rest of the settlement can bloody well take care of themselves.

Just yesterday morning I sat down in the woods with Laughing Boy and tried to tell him about gold.

"It's like stone," I said, holding up a gray pebble from beneath a tree. "Like this, but it is beautiful and bright. Yellow, like the sun." I pointed to the sky, where through bare branches the sun could be seen. "It is what will make me a gentleman, and you, too, if you want."

Laughing Boy crossed his legs and his arms and shook his head. Clearly it made no sense to him.

Then I pointed to the pouch at Laughing Boy's waist. He opened it. I pulled out the blue bead. "Like this," I said. "It is valuable, and everyone wants it. Gold. Men kill and die for it."

Laughing Boy chuckled, jumped to his feet, and ran off after a squirrel.

I realized then that gold-hunting would be something I would have to do alone. Damn it all. It would have been easier with two, especially a Powhatan!

❧ 18 ❧

December 25, 1607–January 1, 1608

WE CAN'T SURVIVE with Wingfield as president,"
said the bushy-haired gentleman Robert Fenton
to the bald gentleman Thomas Sands as the men of
James Towne exited the settlement's church on Christmas afternoon. Those who were well enough to attend
the service did so, but there were a number who had
had to celebrate the morn of Christ's birth from the
darkness of their cabins, for their fevers had stolen
their vitality. The ground was frozen from an early-
morning sleet, the sky was gray, and the air was as cold
and cruel as the blade of a sword. Reverend Hunt had
spoken for hours on the glorious birth of Jesus and the
saintliness of His mother and the love of God, and for
hours the men had recited verses and had sung hymns,
and Nat's back was tired.

"Hush," said Thomas Sands. "Let us talk outside earshot of those who would disagree." The two gentlemen
walked slowly toward the West Bulwark of the fortress.
Nat, a scarf torn from the remnants of a wool blanket
tied around his ears, followed the men. He acted as

though he had business in the pigs' pen, which was only several yards from the bulwark. When he reached the woven fence, he climbed over and proceeded to rearrange the buckets. He was reminded of the times he and Richard had pretended to still have rats to toss into the ocean so they could stay above board longer. There were only two pigs remaining from those brought in May. In the fall the pigs had been allowed to run in the forests to find their own food, but this remaining pair had been brought back to the fort. Many of the laborers suspected that Edward Maria Wingfield was planning a Yuletide feast for himself and some of his closest supporters like Archer and Kendall.

Robert Fenton crossed his arms, leaned against the fortress wall, and spoke in a lowered voice. "John Smith left to explore the Chickahominy River earlier this month, and while he has been gone, Wingfield and his friends have blatantly taken advantage of the rest of us."

Thomas Sands scratched himself beneath the collar of his cloak and then pulled at the curls of his mustache. "Even though he sees the state we are in, even though he sees the very starvation of those he is supposed to govern, he does not expect gentlemen to work. But I work, and you do, as well. We both know now that for even the daintiest man to do nothing is a doom-say for us all. I would rather be a living man than a dead gentleman."

The bushy-haired man agreed. "Wingfield is a fool."

Nat placed the buckets back on the ground and then pretended to reweave a loose branch in the pen fence.

"We should send out a party to find Smith and bring him back," said Sands. "Smith has a clear head when it comes to the needs of our fort. He knows all should work. He knows gentlemen must dirty their hands if they are to live."

Fenton frowned, listening.

Sands continued. "We should bring Smith home to James Towne and settle this once and for all. Let us, as a whole body of Englishmen, gentleman, soldier, surgeon, laborer, all, decide who should govern James Towne. If each man gets a say, I can tell you for certain Wingfield would lose and Smith would be given the presidency of the council."

"Your ideas are radical," said Fenton. "And I understand your anxiousness. But it would be best to wait until Smith returns on his own. This will give us time to talk privately to others and gain their support, so when Smith does indeed show up, we are ready to make our stand. You have heard there is safety in numbers, sir."

"No," said Sands. "If we wait, it will give Wingfield the time to let us all die slow deaths from starvation."

Robert Fenton picked up a stick lying at his feet and hurled it angrily through the air. "Do you hear us, sir? We can't even agree on a simple plan, and yet we are on the same side. How hard will it be to get more than two men to agree to any plan regarding the disposal of Wingfield?"

Suddenly there was a loud squeal, and Nat felt a sharp set of teeth cut through his trousers and into the flesh of his buttocks. "God save me!" he shouted. He jumped out of the fenced enclosure, holding his bleeding wound. One of the pigs eyed him, the animal's lips seeming to be set in a grin.

Thomas Sands rushed at Nat. Nat stumbled back, ready to explain what had happened so the man wouldn't strike him. But Sands only turned Nat around and stared at the ripped breeches and the blood.

"See there," said Sands. "Even our bloody pigs are making a bloody nuisance of themselves, starved as they are in this dreadful land, biting bloody boys in the arse and making bloody messes!"

Robert Fenton looked at the wound, Thomas Sands looked at the wound, and Nat, from over his shoulder, tried to look at the wound. Then all three of them burst out laughing.

"You have adopted the language of the commoner," chuckled Fenton.

"I have indeed!"

"A bloody mess it all is!" said the bushy-haired gentleman. "Bloody fort, bloody savages, bloody diseases!"

"Bloody cold, bloody bad water, bloody Virginia!" said Sands.

"Bloody, damnable Wingfield!" said Nat.

The two men stopped laughing. Thomas Sands spun Nat back around to face him. "Why did you mention our president to us?" he demanded.

"Oh," said Nat, his mind scrambling for an act. "Oh, sir, I beg pardon. Please don't beat me. I meant no disrespect to our good president. I know you men admire him, and I do, too. I'm only speaking because one of these pigs belongs to President Wingfield and I believe the man has taught the pig to bite."

The two men stared at Nat a moment longer, then the soldier let go of Nat's collar. "Well, then, should we just say 'Wingfield's damnable pig'?"

"Of course, sir."

"Fine. Fine." But the men continued to stare at Nat. Then Fenton said, "You are the boy who playacts."

"Yes, sir."

"Who would you entertain us with?"

Nat paused. He wasn't sure who best to act as for these men. If he acted as Smith, like most gentlemen wanted, then they might be offended because they truly liked Smith. But if he acted as someone the commoners hated, such as Wingfield or Archer, then they would know he'd overheard their discussion. "Sir," he said. "My buttocks hurt. Could I do it another time?"

Fenton nodded. "Of course. Go and clean yourself up."

Nat bowed. "Thank you, sir." He hobbled to the well and drew up a small bucketful of icy water. This he dabbed on his wound with a corner of the wool scarf, then inspected the flesh as best he could. It wasn't deep, but it was painful. There was nothing he could do but to wait until it healed. He wrapped the scarf back around his ears and walked out of the fort and down to the river to try to find some shellfish for Christmas dinner.

He tossed rocks into the water to break up the ice at river's edge, but after an hour of poking in the deep mud with a stick, he had caught nothing, and went to bed hungry.

Two days after Christmas, both gentlemen Robert Fenton and Thomas Sands were put into the James Towne jail for, as Wingfield declared, "no less than thirty days." Someone had told the council president that the two gentlemen had spoken against him. Although there were no identified eyewitnesses to the traitorous talk, and all that was spoken against Fenton and Sands was hearsay from an unnamed source, Wingfield declared that an example had to be set.

Nat's tent was not far from the jail, and he had to pass it on his way home at night. He didn't look at the jail because he didn't want to see the faces of the men, pressed to the slats of their tiny windows, gaunt, furious. He knew they believed he had told on them. He knew they believed he was responsible for their confinement.

Neither man spoke to Nat as he went by. But on New Year's Eve, as Nat retired for the evening, he thought he heard Thomas Sands say, "What did you tell for, boy? We were on your side."

And Nat, ever the thespian, acted as if he didn't hear.

And on New Year's Day, John Smith returned to the cheers of many and the silent discontentment of Wingfield and his council.

✤ 19 ✤

January 4, 1608

At last! I have a cottage! Although I must share it with
Samuel Collier, William Love, and John Laydon. It is smaller
than the other cottages, and not much warmer than the rotting
tent, but it is sturdy and the winds will not blow it down. We
caked the walls thick with mud and have woven door and
window mats with dried grasses from outside the fort. There
is one room, with two cots and two mattresses, a single table,
and John Laydon's trunk.

Although I would not have chosen Samuel Collier to share
a home with me, it makes writing convenient. He has a supply
of pens and ink and paper for the times he takes notes for
John Smith. I steal a little every week or so. He is a sluggish,
careless boy. I don't think he has noticed.

I kept the skins of the deer I killed; they help keep the excru-
ciating cold off me. William Love cried out so dreadfully with
shivers three nights ago I covered him with one of the skins to
quiet him. He still has it.

More men of James Towne have died from weakness, foul
water, and little food. Burials are quick now and with little
dignity, performed at night so the natives, who the soldiers
swear are watching us constantly, won't know how few of us

there are. Our scarce crops from summer are rationed to each man, even the lazy gentlemen who never lifted a finger to help acquire this food. We each are given a bit of wheat and beans daily. It is not enough. But I have seen some of the councilors, even our president Edward Maria Wingfield, go into the storehouse and steal away much more than what is rightfully theirs. If they knew I knew of their dishonesty, they would probably banish me.

The food I saved in my sack from the many months here in Virginia went more quickly than I'd hoped. Some had spoiled beyond hope, and the rest was gone as of November. If it weren't for Laughing Boy, I might be dead now, starved like the others. I do not see the Powhatan as often as I did in the autumn; with his pantomime and stick sketches I know he must spend these winter months hunting with his village. But regularly I find a bundle of corn, nuts, and dried meat left for me where I buried the beads. I gorge myself before I return to James Towne.

Now that the gardens are dead for the winter, most of us do not go beyond the fortress. The soldiers still take turns watching for attacks, but sometimes their weakness causes them to doze, leaving us in danger. There has been much rain and sleet and some snow. My feet are sometimes so numb I can barely stand, but I know if I don't move around, it will only be worse. Very few men look to me for humor now, for which I am thankful. It is too cold to joke.

Thomas Sands and Robert Fenton have been released from their imprisonment, with less than thirty days served. I avoid them as best as possible. I do not like the looks in their eyes. It is not hatred, but a near-pity. I do not need anyone's pity. I only need to survive.

As I write with these stiff fingers, I hear weak shouts from outside my cottage. I hear, "Susan Constant." Susan Constant! The ship has arrived! There will be supplies, food, clothing, weapons. I stop for now.

✌ 20 ✌

January 7–30, 1608

NAT DREAMED OF London, of a stable where he and Richard and another London boy Matthew used to hide when it was cold and rainy. He could smell the scent of clean horses and could feel the warmth of the dusty, brittle straw. Richard and Matthew were nearby, sitting around a small fire, cooking fish scraps and a plump pigeon. Nicholas Skot was there, too, and sitting behind him was Samuel Collier, and one of the new boys, thirteen-year-old Thomas Savage. Boys all waiting for a meal. Nat could feel his mouth water, anticipating the tasty flesh.

But then a spark jumped from the fire and landed in the straw near Nat. "Watch out!" said Richard. Nat tried to get up and away, but his legs were frozen. The straw burst into flames, leaping up and licking the side of Nat's face. Matthew shouted, "Nat, get away now!"

Nat's arms flailed out trying to push the fire back, but still he couldn't stand. The hair on his head began to sizzle. The skin on his face began to melt.

"Get out!"

Get out!

Nat's eyes flew open to the black of night and the shouts of John Laydon in the open doorway. "Nathaniel, Samuel, William, get out! There's fire in the fort!"

In a second he was off his mattress and into his shoes. There was a smell of ash in the cottage, pungent and strong. It stung his eyes. Nat stumbled outside into the frigid night. Samuel and William fell out behind him.

The fort was in an uproar. On the south corner of the fort, Nat could see bright towers of orange-red flames. Cottages were on fire, their reed-covered roofs engulfed, their windows belching smoke. Men raced to the wells, tossing down buckets on ropes and hauling them up again, then running to hurl the water on the structures. There were shouts of panic, there were wails of despair. Many of the voices belonged to the new settlers who had arrived just three days earlier with the supplies and had bedded down in crowded cottages until new homes could be built.

"God help us, why have we come here?"

"We should never have sailed to Virginia!"

"We are doomed!"

"Lord, pity!" said Samuel. "We'll lose everything."

The winter wind was intense, blowing across the tops of the burning cottages and throwing flame tongues onto the buildings next to them.

John Smith, his face blacked with soot, came over to Nat and Samuel and gave each one a sharp smack to the head. "What are you doing there? Go to the river with anything to carry water. I won't have you standing about like simpletons! Hurry!"

Nat darted back into his cottage and grabbed his sack. It might leak, but perhaps it would hold water long enough to get some back to the fort. Samuel followed him, taking up his own smaller sack. They made their way through the chaos within the fort and down the frozen, slippery bank to the river.

The water's edge was covered with a layer of ice. Nat drove his foot through the ice, lost his balance, and stepped into the shallows.

The cold was like a knife to his legs. But he grabbed a handful of grass and pulled himself out. Then he dragged the sack through the water and lugged it back up the slope. Samuel complained the whole way. "A sack can't carry water, mine is leaking. So is yours. This is absurd!"

"Be quiet, boy," said Nat.

There was half a sack of water by the time Nat reached the first burning cottage. A tall man grabbed the sack from him and dumped the water through a smoking window. Then Nat went back to the river.

He lost track of the number of times he ran up and down the slope with his sack. His frozen legs tried to lock up under him, but he pushed them onward. He was aware that Samuel was sometimes beside him, sometimes not, but mostly he was aware of the smells of smoke and the smells of fear. Men shouted, their words no longer intelligible but animal shrieks of terror and anguish.

"We're all going to die!"

"God curse you, London Company, for sending us to our deaths here in this terrible place!"

There was a hazy red glow in the east by the time the fires were at last extinguished. The sun was coming up over the river, its light burning the sky like a cold, taunting fire. Now the damage was visible. Many cottages were destroyed, their grass-and-reed roofs and mud-and-stick walls nothing but smoldering ruins.

The men gathered in the remains of the church, those who had come in 1607 and those who had arrived on the *Susan Constant* just days prior, all looking much the same in their angst and worry, dropping down on charred benches and looking at the ground as if the earth had the answers they sought. The roof was half gone, and just three of the four walls still stood. It was as though God and the devil themselves had battled here, each one trying to claim this house of worship. Nat hated to think it, but it looked as though the devil had given the Lord quite a challenge.

"Where is God?" one man near Nat wondered aloud. "Why has He brought us here for this? We are not as pious as Job, so why must we be tested as severely?"

The Reverend Hunt preached for many hours. He raised his hands to heaven and sought God's help in enduring the difficulties of Virginia. He led the men in the singing of songs and reciting of Psalms, but most of the voices were now scratchy and faint with the ravages of smoke. Reverend Hunt thanked God for the lives and buildings that were spared in the fire. The minister's face and hands were black with ash, and his robe was scorched, yet his words were earnest and sincere.

"Our blessed Redeemer, give us courage to continue our mission here in the New World!"

Most of the men answered, "Amen." Some said nothing.

Over the weeks that followed, the James Towne men worked to rebuild, but this time in wind cold enough to cut flesh. Chopping trees to replace the cottages and plastering frozen mud for walls made joints and muscles ache. At times Nat felt his hands would break off the ends of his arms like brittle icicles. The settlers had so little strength it took three times as long to build a cottage as it had in the summer. Everyone's faces— John Laydon, Samuel Collier, John Smith, Nicholas Skot, and all the others—seemed to have shrunken into skulls. Cheekbones protruded, eyes were hollow and dark, lips were dry, cracked, and often bloody.

I suppose I look as they do, Nat wrote one night as he sat on his mattress after John Laydon had extinguished the lantern and the glow of the moon through the window was the only light available. *It is a good thing I am not wealthy enough to own a looking glass. What a fright I would have.*

Laydon was in his silent prayers now, his eyes closed, his body trembling. Samuel lay on his own mattress, facing away from Nat. Nat hadn't heard Samuel utter more than a few words since the fire. He went to Smith's cottage when called, but other than that, was distant and withdrawn. Maybe he was sick, although Nat had not heard the rasping cough that the dying men had. Maybe he had just given up hope for a good life in Virginia. Maybe he just wanted to go home to England.

Nat looked back at his paper, and couldn't think of anything else to write. He covered the page with one of his remaining deerskins. Then he drew his knees up to his chest and forced himself to sleep.

He awoke when it was still dark, although he could feel the coming morning in the air. His stomach growled, still believing it could demand a meal. Beneath his sack was the sharpened stick Laughing Boy had given him to fish. If he went down to the river now, no one would question him. Even though fish were hard to find in the winter, perhaps he could stir up something in the frosty water.

Quietly he pulled on his stiff shoes and cloak, then went out of the cottage and through the center of the fort toward the gate. Men could be heard through the windows of their cottages, snoring, coughing, and moaning. *What are their dreams?* Nat wondered. The watch in the bulwarks were clearly sleeping; no one stirred as he moved the large wooden post from the latch of the gate and slipped outside.

The stars in the sky were beginning to grow fuzzy as the sun in the east found a fingerhold on the horizon. Pale gray sunlight crawled across the river and the distant trees. Nat knew it would bring no warmth, however. He reached his boulder and stood with the spear raised, staring into the water, watching for a splash.

There was rustling in the trees along the clearing. Nat spun around. Walking softly, sneaking toward the fort, was an entire band of natives.

Nat's mouth opened, but nothing came out. The spear fell from his hands. He took a deep breath and screamed, "Muskets! Quickly, muster now, for the savages are coming!"

His legs loosened and he dashed up the frozen path to the fort's gate. He knew arrows would be flying in just a moment; he knew he would be the first one dead when the natives drew their bows.

But Nat stumbled once, and as he righted himself he looked over his shoulder. The natives were still walking to the fort, but none had bows or other weapons readily at hand. Instead, their arms and shoulders were laden with turkeys, whole deer and some half carcasses, and baskets of dried vegetables, nuts, and corn.

Nat stopped and stared.

At the front of the line skipped a young girl, a bit younger than himself, wearing a deerskin dress decorated in shells and feathers. Her black hair was bound in leather thongs at the back of her neck. Around her neck was a single blue glass bead. She was smiling.

The remaining Powhatans were men, bearing the food. Their faces were solemn but not threatening. They seemed determined to do the job they had come to do. Deliver food.

Unless it's a trick, Nat thought. *Like the Trojan horse,*

*perhaps they are hiding hatchets and clubs in those baskets,
ready to kill us if we let them into the fort!*

And then Nat saw someone near the rear of the procession, someone he knew. It was Laughing Boy. He
carried a skin bundle filled with ears of dry corn. The
boy nodded at Nat, barely, though, as if he didn't want
the others to know that he and Nat were acquain-
tances. *Good*, thought Nat. *If the men of James Towne knew
I spent time with a native, they would punish me severely.*

It was only then that the watch came awake in the
murky morning light, and began to scream, "Muskets!
Muster quickly, we are under attack! All men, muster!"

The cannons on the bulwarks squeaked as they were
positioned. Inside the walls, men could be heard shouting, "Attack! We are under attack! Hurry!"

But Nat cried, "They have brought food for us!
Wait!"

A soldier at the cannon cried, "Shut up, boy!"

But Nat insisted. "Look, please! They've got food!"

The soldier straightened from the cannon and held
up a hand. "Wait, the boy is right! Hold your muskets,
men. We have a friendly visit!"

The fort gate swung open and John Smith came out,
dressed already in his best uniform. Even his hat was
placed carefully on his head and it seemed as if his
beard had been combed. Nat had never known anyone
who could look so dignified and so in command at
such short notice. Surely the man had been sound
asleep only a minute earlier.

"Pocahontas!" said Smith, sweeping his arms wide
and welcoming the girl. "Welcome to James Towne,
and to all those with you. Come in!"

He stood back, his cape flapping, and the natives
entered the fort. Nat let them pass, glancing only once
at Laughing Boy. As he did, Laughing Boy pointed to
the hollow of his throat and tipped his head toward

the front of the procession. Nat knew immediately what he was saying. Laughing Boy had given Pocahontas the blue bead. But why?

Everyone was up now, except the men too ill to leave their lodgings. John Smith gathered everyone around and waved his arms. "As I have told the council, because of my travels into the wilderness of Virginia and my visits to many Powhatan villages, we would someday have a time of peace between the natives and ourselves. That time has come. And the daughter of the great Chief Powhatan, Pocahontas, has initiated this feast before us. We are grateful to her for her generosity and pray our people will from this day forward share the land in tranquility."

Pocahontas beamed as John Smith bowed to her. She spun her arms around as if in dance, then said something to the natives behind her. They placed the foods on the ground. Even the most distrustful of the settlers at last laid down their muskets and collected the baskets and the meats. Nat took a small deer, threw it over his shoulder, and followed the other Englishmen to the storehouse. The animals would be skinned and then smoked dry to be eaten over the rest of the winter. The other foods, already prepared, would be rationed out by the councilors until spring.

John Smith conversed with the princess, using those words he knew of her language and a series of gestures. Clearly he wanted Pocahontas to thank her father for sending the food. Nat let his gaze wander over to Laughing Boy, who stood with his arms crossed. Carefully, so not to attract anyone else's attention, Laughing Boy pointed toward the storehouse and then to his forehead. He then touched his neck, nodded at Pocahontas, and shook his head. At last he patted his stomach and pointed at Nat.

Nat understood. It wasn't Pocahontas who had decided to bring food to the settlers. It was Laughing Boy's idea. He knew the settlers were starving. But Laughing Boy had no status to make such a grand proposal. And so he had given Pocahontas the blue glass bead, a rare and wonderful gift, so she would make the arrangements. But for some reason, Laughing Boy didn't really mind that the girl got the thanks, not him.

After Pocahontas and the natives had gone and the sun was up fully, fires were struck to heat up a fine meal of corn and venison. Men sat about, rubbing their hands against the warmth and loudly chewing the meat from the animal bones.

"This is a blessing from God," said Reverend Hunt to John Smith. "The Lord has seen fit to stir the hearts of the savages in order for us to live again."

"Thank God and thank me," said Smith, his mouth full of corn. "The Lord has given me the talent to ease the minds of the savages. I doubt any other settler would have had this effect on their dark hearts. And Pocahontas was so pleased with the appreciation we showed, she will come again."

President Edward Maria Wingfield sat near enough to Nat to be overheard saying, "Smith thanks God for the glory of being Smith. Those savages are never to be trusted." He cracked open the leg bone of a deer and began to suck the marrow from within. "I could see the treachery in their eyes even as they were handing us this food."

Gabriel Archer said, "True. Smith is so bloated with his own sense of worth he would pop if he ran into a thorn." Archer patted the dagger on his belt. "He best watch out for my thorn."

Wingfield nodded seriously and John Ratcliffe put his hand to his mouth to stifle a chuckle. Nat stared at the portion of deer leg in his hands. He pretended not to hear the councilors' discussion.

21

February 16, 1608

The new boy Thomas Savage is gone from us, traded to Powhatan as a hostage just a month after his arrival at James Towne. Smith and Newport ushered Thomas and his chest of clothing from us, and far up the river. They returned with a savage to live with us and learn our language. I did not know Thomas well, but that he was a tall boy for thirteen, and silent and respectful to gentlemen. So I do not think I shall miss him, but a cold chill ran down me when, again, I saw how easily a boy is gotten rid of. The savage who came to James Towne with Smith is a little older than I, but not much. His name is Namontack. He spends his time with the carpenters and with Reverend Hunt, learning how we build, how we speak, and how we pray. Newport plans to take him back to England. I will have nothing to do with him, not knowing how to trust him or if I should even want to.

Perhaps Thomas will find Richard and Richard will not be so alone in the wilderness. Perhaps, if Richard is still living.

Perhaps.

The New World is full of perhaps.

❧ 22 ❧

April 30, 1608

    Pocahontas comes to our fort several times a week, bringing food and taking messages from John Smith to her father, the great Powhatan. The girl is haughty, bold, but I have a respect for her that I did not have earlier. She does indeed face danger when she comes to our fort. How can she know we won't act abruptly as her people sometimes do? Englishmen can be savage, though most would not admit it.

    We are growing stronger with the victuals and the warmer weather. Our moods are a bit improved, though the damage from the fire is not totally repaired yet, and there are still many graves around the settlement.

    Sometimes Laughing Boy comes with the delivery of food, sometimes not. I've often wondered how I could ask him about Richard, if he's seen him, if he is still alive. But our communication is still so limited, I doubt I will ever be able to convey my concerns. And I don't really know if I want to know the truth. What if Richard has been tortured to death, burned or gored?

    We have begun planting our gardens once more. It is not long until we celebrate our first anniversary in James Towne. Celebrate. Not quite the word I should use. But this year could be better. *The natives have given us some seeds to help us with our farming.*

Amazingly, Thomas Savage was not slaughtered by the Powhatans, but has learned enough of their language to act as liaison at some of the trading expeditions Smith has taken over the past two months. I suppose, then, that he is faring well. Or as well as a child can in the face of everything strange and wild. God knows, I do not envy him. How the world, how circumstance, can turn in but a moment.

The *Susan Constant* sailed twenty days ago, back to England, talking some wood to the Company and collecting some more supplies for us. We've got no gold yet. I doubt wood will please the Company much.

We've got men making glass now, fancy, delicate green vessels for candles and beer. The sand along the riverside is melted down to create these wares.

But no gold.

Not a bit of gold.

🐝 23 🐝

September 28–October 12, 1608

IT WAS WITH mixed feelings that the men of James Towne had greeted the arrival of more settlers on September 20. There were supplies of food and tools and crates of pigs and goats, for which everyone was thrilled. But like the 120 who had come to James Towne in April of this year, the new men who arrived in September were no more knowledgeable of the way of the wilds than were the first settlers to arrive on the *Susan Constant*, the *Godspeed*, and the *Discovery* over a year ago. The Virginia Company had been angry that no gold had been sent from the New World to England, and they were determined to make sure gold was forthcoming. Instead of carpenters and farmers, which James Towne needed greatly, the Company sent gold refiners and more glassmakers. The new council president, John Ratcliffe, seemed at a loss as to how to manage so many people. He shouted orders, whipped those laborers he felt were disrespectful or had them tossed into the fort's tiny, thatched jail, and stomped around with his head held high as if he were in control, but he was not. John Smith was. Men moved more quickly for Smith than Ratcliffe, a fact not lost on the council president.

More trees were cleared from the surrounding forest and houses were built outside the fort. The ground was scraped to make additional fall gardens in which to raise pumpkins and winter wheat, though most of the newcomers had no idea of how to work a crop. Nat thought James Towne was beginning to sound and smell like London.

But there was something new and curious which had come on the ship from England this time. There were two women. One was a married lady named Lucy Forrest, a tall and quiet woman who spoke only with permission of her husband, Thomas. The other was a young girl named Ann Burras. She was Mistress Forrest's servant girl, and there was nothing quiet about her at all. In her mistress's presence, she was obedient and humble. But when she was off about her duties around the fort, drawing water and washing clothes and emptying chamber pots, she chattered to herself nonstop, complaining about the filthy conditions of James Towne and the constant stares of the men who lived there.

On one sunny afternoon as Nat was patching the walls of the church, he felt a dig in his ribs. He dropped the bucket of mud and it fell to its side with a clatter.

"Oh, I am sorry!" It was Ann, her hands on her hips, her nose wrinkled. A lock of hair had fallen from beneath the hood of her cape. "I meant to tease, not frighten."

"I'm not frightened," said Nat. "But you must learn that here in Virginia there are many things which can startle a man. Often it is a savage with a knife to slit the Englishman's throat or a club of bone to smash in his brains. You are lucky I didn't take you for a savage or I would have thrown you to the ground and stomped your neck."

Ann's blue eyes grew wide and her lips twitched. "Sir, you speak so cruelly to me!"

"No, I speak honestly."

Ann's eyebrows drew together in suspicion. But then she smiled. "You are a strong, honest man, I can see that." Then she tossed her head and strolled off.

Nat made a point of speaking to her every day after that. He watched her as she worked with Mistress Forrest washing clothes and preparing meals over the fire outside their house. He helped her carry water and gave her his last deer hide. In spite of her nasal voice, she was not an ugly girl at all.

"Winters in Virginia are harsh," he told Ann one evening at the riverside. "Many men starved last year."

"How dreadful."

"It is true," said Nat. "You need only see the graves to know what we endured."

Ann scowled and looked away across the river.

"But," Nat continued, "I'm a good hunter. I can always get more. In fact, I am a true survivor here. I have a secret supply of treasure in the forest."

Ann looked back at Nat, her eyes widening. She glanced around to make sure no one was gazing in her direction, and gave Nat a quick kiss on the cheek.

That evening, as Nat sat on his mattress removing his shoes, John Laydon said, "Miss Burras is pretty, isn't she?"

Nat shrugged. "I haven't noticed," he said. Had John seen the kiss? Probably not. Most of the men thought Ann pretty. But it made Nat feel self-conscious, regardless.

"Play a role for me," said John. "You are our town's

actor, young Peacock. How would Ann act if a man were to ask her to marry him?"

"Do you want a farce or a drama?" asked Nat.

"I'll leave that up to you."

Samuel said, "So you think you can act as a woman?"

William Love, bending over a torn linen shirt, said, "Let's see comedy!"

Nat pursed his lips and ran his fingers through his tangled hair. His eyebrows peaked as he said, "Oh, sir, you ask me for my hand? I am so flattered, but, sir, you are an old man, old enough to be my father! So I must decline, but I thank you warmly for your offer."

Samuel rolled his eyes. William Love laughed. But John Laydon didn't seem amused.

Over the next few days, Ann made a point of waving to Nat and speaking to him. She stopped her complaining when she was near him, and she seemed to make of point of smoothing her skirts and tucking her hair carefully when she saw him coming in her direction.

After worship service in the church on a pleasant afternoon, Ann pulled Nat aside and said, "Show me the treasure you have in the forest."

Nat felt his cheeks go red. He hadn't meant to tell anyone about the place where Laughing Boy, now that autumn had set in, had begun once more to leave food and symbols of peace between the two of them every ten days. Some days Laughing Boy would be there with the gift and he and Nat would go exploring or hunting. Other times the Powhatan only left the gift. But what if Ann saw Laughing Boy in the forest and was terrified? What if she thought food was not truly treasure? Could Nat trust her?

But she smiled and took his arm, and Nat knew it would be all right.

Ann had to wait until early the next morning, when her mistress thought she was washing clothes in the river. She and Nat crept through the tall stalks of un-harvested corn and entered the forest.

Immediately Ann seemed uncomfortable. "It's too hard to walk. My shoes are not for such rough ground."

"Watch your step," said Nat. "You'll get used to it."

Ann said, "Humph," and held the hem of her skirt to keep it off the briars. She kept close to Nat, grabbing his shoulder when her balance teetered and grumbling. "Why would you have treasure so far out here? What good is it if you can't grab it up when you want to look at it?"

Nat said nothing.

"Is it gold? Silver? Pearls, perhaps!" said Ann.

Nat felt his teeth grind together. Pearls? This was a mistake. She had never been hungry, even if she was a mere servant girl.

"Nathaniel, where is the treasure? What is it?"

Nat stopped and said, "There is the treasure, Ann." On the ground, wrapped in large sycamore leaves, was a gift of several small squash, three ears of corn, and some beautiful red-gold feathers. "I have lived in Virginia for more than a year. I've learned that there are other treasures besides gold. Food is more precious. Someday I'll find gold, but for now, I give thanks for food. And there, beneath that pile of stones, are five blue glass beads. Worthless to either of us in England, but like money here, I have them hidden in case I find need to give one to the natives. They find them exquisite."

Ann tilted her head and chuckled for a second. Nat thought she would think about it for a moment and then realize what he was saying was true. But her face drew in and she frowned. "Surely you are teasing me," she said. "Now, where is the real treasure?"

Nat put an ear of corn in Ann's hand. "Here. Look at it. It is gold-colored, is it not? And it is smooth like gold. I am given gifts of food regularly, and I hide them in my sack in my cottage until the worst of times. In my sack now are many ears of corn. This way I do not have to depend on the other men of James Towne."

"I thought you were a rich man."

"In a way I am."

"Where does this food come from?"

"A Powhatan boy."

"Powhatan? You mean a savage?"

"Yes," said Nat. "But he is truly not savage."

Ann gave the corn back but said nothing.

Three days later, John Laydon caught Nat by the arm as he was tossing grain to the pigs. "I have a deal for you, comedian. You give me the sack of victuals you have been hiding in our cottage and the glass beads you have buried in the woods, and I won't tell John Smith that you stole from him and have been illegally keeping food to yourself. That will be your death, boy, and you know I tell the truth."

Nat gave John the sack, and the man put it in his trunk. He took John into the forest and dug up the beads. Four weeks later, John and Ann Burras were married in the church with the blessing of Mistress Forrest and Reverend Hunt and under the jealous eye of a couple hundred lonely men.

❧ 24 ❧

December 30, 1608

John Smith has done it again! Samuel Collier was taken on an expedition to the native village of Waraskoyack, and did not return with the men. I heard from Edward Pising that John Smith left Samuel with Powhatan, "assuring the king perpetual love," in order to keep the peace and for Samuel to learn the language. Someday, Pising says, Samuel may come back to us with this knowledge, and, as with Thomas Savage, we will all benefit. I did not know Thomas Savage, but I knew Richard. I knew Samuel. And for all the page's irritable spirits, I would not have wished this upon him.

Nicholas Skot has told me he is afraid he will be next to be taken away, and asked me what he should do. I told him I do not know. Just as we are unable to tell when we offend the Powhatans and bring attack upon ourselves or when we please them and bring about assistance, I am unable to know the heart and mind of John Smith when it comes to matters such as the trading of boys.

I do not hate Smith as the councilors do, but I do not revere him the way the commoners do. His turn has come to be president of the James Towne council and he is a harsher ruler than the others, which is to our benefit. He makes everyone work. *Those not hunting or collecting food are set to building and repairing our homes and the fort walls or splitting logs and putting them on ships to sail for England in a few days.*

But regardless, I cannot stomach the man as I once did.

Smith visits the natives and trades for food when the storehouse supplies grow slim. I think he enjoys the adventure a bit too much, leaving most of us behind to labor. I wonder if he misses the beads I took. I wonder if, on his trips, he has seen Richard. I have asked him, but he ignored me, as if such a matter is past and should remain past. Pocahontas, the young Powhatan girl, still comes on occasion with baskets of food. We are not starving as we did the last winter, and though I avoid Smith, I do give him credit for his steadfast control. He even makes everyone, from carpenter to sailor to tailor to gentleman, drill with muskets daily so we might be better ready if we are attacked again. Captains Archer and Wingfield obey, but they secretly rebel by continuing to steal from the storehouse when no one is around. I doubt I am the only one who has seen them sneaking out with food under their cloaks, but no one yet seems up to challenging them. They must remember the man who was executed for treason our first summer. Accusing our leaders would be nearly as bad as speaking against the king.

William Love seems pleased to have chores other than hunting and fishing. With many new men now, he is busy with tailoring, mending clothes and stitching new trousers from the small stock of fabric which arrived from London. He is not much with a musket. He can't even hit a tree stump. But he does have talent with a needle.

John Laydon and his wife have a cottage to themselves now. I am certain Ann is enjoying the little extra food which was my very reluctant wedding gift. I believe I even saw the blue beads around her neck, hiding just beneath her collar. John and Ann watch me like hawks, seeing if I try to go again into the woods alone. I've not been back since October. A handful of extra food is not worth the hangman's noose. I hope John is happy with Mistress Laydon. He can have her. I wish him luck with such a spiteful girl.

My shoes have holes in them. They won't last another year.

25

June 3–27, 1609

NAT HAD THOUGHT that, once off the *Susan Constant*, his duty of rat-catcher was over. But it wasn't.

The first of the garden's yields came in early June, and the storehouses were filled with potatoes, peas, and radishes. Other crops had been planted now, the corn, squash, beans, and cabbages, which, if all went well, would be ready to harvest in August. It was hot, but there were still occasional cool mornings and evenings, making it seem as though spring had forgotten its time was done. Sometimes, in the early days of June, the men would find themselves feeling more merry than usual, and a gentleman would pull out the flute he'd carried over on the ship and play a happy, dancing tune.

Nat even found his own feet tapping to the music as he sat at the edge of the gatherings. Yes, he knew there was gold still to be found. Perhaps it didn't sit on the top of the soil as he'd thought, perhaps it wasn't glittering in the fields or sparkling in the streams, but it was there, certainly. Underground, maybe. In a cave, at the bottom of a pond or lake. But it was there. And Nat knew that once James Towne had grown strong and no longer had to fight daily for a piece of bread, then there would be time for him to go exploring once more. This time he'd take a shovel.

But then, on a morning in the middle of the month, as the men gathered at the door to the storehouse for their rations of vegetables and last year's corn, there was a shout of dismay.

"Rats!"

"Damn the vermin! They've helped themselves to our store!"

"How dreadful!" said Ann Laydon.

Nat stood on tiptoe to peer over the shoulder of the tall man in front of him. He could see inside the shadowy store, and indeed the place was alive with the creatures. How could they have gotten in and multiplied so quickly in just a week? There had been a few times when the storehouse had borne vermin, but only in small numbers and found before much damage could be done. But this time it seemed as if a sea of rats were swimming in the stock, crawling over and under barrels and crates and in and out of cracks they had gnawed into the wood.

"Back up," demanded John Smith. The men backed up. Smith motioned for Nicholas Skot, who came up reluctantly. His hair hadn't seen a comb in many weeks, and looked like a greasy tangle of seaweed.

"Boy," said Smith. "You and Peacock are assigned to rid this place of the rats. I want every one gone by dusk."

And so Nat and Nicholas were on rat duty. With clubs in hand, they crept through the crates and barrels of food, smacking rats and tossing them out the door. Nicholas said, "Why do we not just shoot the damnable things?" but Nat reminded him what would happen if a matchlock musket caused a spark in the storehouse. A rat infestation would seem like nothing compared to a roaring blaze.

The rats had done serious damage. They had chewed holes into the crates and barrels and had been living inside, eating their fills and leaving rat droppings everywhere. Much of the food was ruined, because it was impossible to separate urine-soaked corn from the dry, the feces-coated peas from the clean.

"I hate rats!" said Nicholas as several ran across his feet and he batted them into heaven.

"And they hate us," said Nat.

By dark, there were still rats in the storehouse, and so Nat and Nicholas were up early the next morning to continue the job. They whacked the creatures as they ran, crushing them beneath the clubs. Nicholas, rolling a barrel over to check for more, was suddenly pounced on by a large, gray creature that ran up his leg to his face.

"God!" he screamed.

The rat bit his cheek before Nat could slap the rat away and crush him beneath his boot.

"I'll have rabies!" cried Nicholas, dropping his club and holding his face in both hands. "God help me!"

"God help you," said Nat. Nicholas was right. There was no telling if he would die from the bite or if it would just take the course of a swelling.

At last the place was rat-free, and the bodies of full-grown rats and clusters of dead baby rats were taken into the woods and pitched. Nat, with a sense of sour humor, nearly asked Nicholas if he wanted to have a rat-tossing contest, but decided against it. But as the last rat crashed into the undergrowth, he said, "It is possible that those creatures will one day look tasty. That the time will come when we wish we had rats for a meal, and hadn't been so hasty as to throw them away."

Nicholas wiped away a tear and returned to the fort.

Nat didn't go back into the fortress immediately, but down to the river, where some of the sailors had launched the shallop. Smith, as usual, stood by supervising, his hands and his hips and his head tilted proudly. He spied Nat and called him over.

"Peacock!" he said. "You boasted at many skills when first we met. I've got men going to Point Comfort to fish. We must have something to fill our bellies. Are you a fisherman as well as farmer, soldier, cook, and carpenter?"

"Yes, sir," Nat said cautiously.

"Then climb aboard and take an oar. I expect you to return with nothing less than brimming buckets."

Nat's stomach clenched. "Is this truly a fishing trip, sir, not an expedition of exploration?"

Smith didn't seem to notice the hesitation in Nat's voice. "Yes, to the Point, or haven't you noticed we need food? Get aboard!"

Nat climbed into the shallop and was given a place near the back. He'd not left James Towne by boat in a long time. It might have been a pleasant change if he was not aware that this might be more than a fishing expedition. It might be another trip of human trade.

But the shallop did indeed row for the Point down the river at the mouth of the bay. Gulls followed the shallop, seeming to think that these men had something they might want. After a half hour of circling, they went off to another adventure. Nat's arms, much stronger and tougher after two years in Virginia, had no trouble working his oar through the water of the James.

The men landed on the sandy beach, hopping out into the small waves of the waist-high water and pulling the shallop half ashore. A sailor named Jonas and other named John drew out the huge net and spread it on the beach, inspecting it for tangles and tears. The other men took their shoes off and put them in the tall grasses, laid their muskets beside their shoes, and then joined in the stitching of the tears. As Nat and John nimbly knotted the thin ropes back into place, Jonas said, "Ye think the shallop would take us back to England safely?"

The men chuckled. "Aye," said John. "Let's board now and we'll be home to our families in, what, three or four years, ye think?"

"Let's be off then!" said Jonas.

And then John hit the beach on his belly, and motioned the others to do so as well. Into the sand he sputtered, "Lord help us, its savages!"

There were curses and swearing, and the men looked helplessly at the muskets they had left by their shoes.

Nat could see them now. There were two canoes, each with four or five natives, paddling south past the Point. Who were they? Where did they come from? Were they the Indians from Cape Henry? Were they from farther north, or perhaps up the James River itself? There was too much distance to see their costumes clearly.

"Does it matter?" Nat muttered to himself. "If they see us, we are dead."

"Ye've got a pistol, John," whispered Jonas.

"Oh," said John into the sand. "And you think I'll take the lot of them with one pistol? I'll kill one or two, and by then they will have come to shore with arrows and hatchets at the ready."

"I mean in case they see us, fool," said Jonas.

"Hush!"

The Englishmen lay as still as they could. It was

worthless, Nat knew, because the shallop was huge and couldn't be missed, sitting there on the beach like a dead whale. It was just a matter of a few more seconds.

And then, as the faces in the canoes turned to stare at the shallop, Nat thought he recognized one of those faces. It was tanned, but seemed to not be of a native, but of a white man. An Englishman. An English boy.

Impossible.

"They've spied us, Jonas!" said John. "What are we to do?"

"Lie still and wait. We've got no other options!"

Impossible, Nat thought. *I'm only imagining things. I want Richard to be alive and so have allowed the sun on the water to play tricks on my mind.*

Either divine or some other mystical providence must have smiled, because the natives continued to steer their canoes, watching, yet doing nothing else, until they could no longer be seen.

"They were afraid," said Jonas, jumping up and brushing off his trousers. "They know of the strength of the Englishmen!"

"They felt sorry for us," said John, grasping the repaired net and walking it to the edge of the water. "They decided we weren't worth the bother."

There was chuckling again, but this time is wasn't as hearty.

And as the men took the net into the briny waters to reap, hopefully, a harvest better than what they'd gleaned from the earth outside the fort at James Towne, all Nat could think about was Richard. Had that been he? Or had it been an illusion?

He threw himself into the fishing to try to forget. To not know.

But the fish the crew took back to James Towne three days later was much less than desired.

❧ 26 ❧

July 4, 1609

God help me, did I see Richard on the bay or was I dreaming? I can't know anymore. Sometimes my mind is muddled with fatigue and hunger, and it makes me want to rip something apart to get away from it! I can't bear feeling out of control! I can't bear feeling my mind is playing tricks on me!

Sometimes when no one is looking, I slap my own face to bring my mind back around to myself. I see the same numbness on the faces of others, too, and it angers me to succumb as they are!

This is our third summer here in Virginia, and we have gone into it with less strength, less vigor, less health and hope than any summer prior, and I fear unless a miracle occurs, we face a winter which could well be our last. As a body needs reserves of fat to live, a soul needs reserves of faith. There is little faith in James Towne. Old and new settlers alike talk among themselves, longing to go back to England, longing to abandon the cottages and fort and let the woods grow back to reclaim it.

Rats are in the storehouse again, but neither Nicholas—who did not die of rabies from the rat bite but whose face grew like a bloated tomato and then subsided to leave it somewhat *lopsided and loose—I, nor any other boy here has been put to chasing them and killing them. As most of us are considered in fair health, we are needed to keep watch and tend gardens and make repairs on cottages which mold and rot before our very eyes. And so, what little grain is scraped from the storehouse barrels and from off the floor is cooked up as it is, with the rat droppings boiled in with the food.*

Men are ill, writhing in agony in their sweat-soaked beds. Two died yesterday. This morning another died.

John Smith demands everyone but those who are on the brink of death be up and wielding muskets and axes and fishing nets. He threatens constantly, mustering everyone together each morning by the door of the church to lecture us and wave his hands at us as his cape billows behind him like the great hand of God. I have witnessed Smith draw up the sick and wheezing Edward Pising from his bed and push the man, stumbling, out of the fort and into the garden beyond to hoe a patch of peas.

A miracle is what we need!

Who told us there was gold here? Piss on him! If there was some to be had, I wonder how it would taste on the tongue. I wonder how it would feel in the belly.

❦ 27 ❦

August 11–12, 1609

SAMUEL COLLIER RETURNED to James Towne in
July at the request of John Smith, not flayed or half
dead but seeming healthy and tattooed with some
marks peculiar to the Powhatans. His red hair was cut
short and the blemishes on his face had disappeared.
He had gained a fair knowledge of the language of the
natives but had lost his curt personality, and a cautious
silence had taken its place. Nat was not displeased to
see his old hut-mate, but Samuel seemed to have less
interest in complaining about day-to-day events, which
took much of the fun out of having the page around.
Samuel moved back into Nat's hut, but spent most of
his time by Smith's side, sharing what he had learned.
Nat picked up some words which he hoped to try out
secretly with Laughing Boy if the chance came, *win-
gapo*—"welcome," *chespin*—"land," *rawcosowghs*—"days,"
toppqough—"nights," *netoppew*—"friends," but refused to
directly ask that Samuel tutor him. One night, when
he could no longer hold his question, he called to Samuel from his cot, "Did you see Richard Mutton among

the natives? He has been gone a long time, but I wonder if he is still alive."

"No," said Samuel matter-of-factly. "I did not see him. There are at least thirty-two tribes under the Powhatan. Forget Richard. His fate is known only to God."

Gabriel Archer left Virginia in midsummer, back to England to obtain more settlers and supplies, but the ever-arrogant Edward Maria Wingfield was still in the settlement, and Nat often saw him huddling together with the young gentleman George Percy down by the river as if they were plotting. Smith had not been hanged back in the West Indies as planned. Would these men try again to take revenge against the captain? Would they strangle Smith in the night? Would they stab Smith behind the storehouse?

Heat, flies, bad food, and jealousy were a perilous combination.

Pocahontas, who had visited the fort throughout the spring of the year, had not been back in a while. Nat wondered if the Powhatans were angry once more with the Englishmen. It was difficult to know when they would be friendly and when they would not, although John Smith had usually been able to make temporary peace with his ability to converse and reason. The Powhatans had different views on the use of land. According to Smith and now Samuel, they believed that the land could not be owned by anyone, that one might as well try to buy the sky and the sun. And so fear or anger would break out and there would be an attack. To most of the settlers, it seemed as if the natives acted on whim alone, but Nat knew English behavior must seem like whim to the natives. It was a relationship that seemed to have no clear answers. And the Englishmen, once again, were forced to rely on their own food supplies.

Nat had become an experienced gardener. He knew how deep to dig for planting beans and peas. He knew how to tend the new stalks of corn so they wouldn't shrivel. He knew which insects would eat the plants and which would eat other insects. The men who had survived from the first year as well as the newer settlers watched him and listened to his advice.

"I beg your pardon, sir! Don't pour that on the corn," he shouted as one little bearded silversmith tipped over a bucket of water he'd drawn from the James River. "It's got salt in it. It will stunt the growth. It is best if you use well water."

The silversmith snarled, "Preposterous. We can't spare well water for plants. We need it for drinking."

"We need corn, sir. Please fill your bucket with well water."

The man drew up his face as if he wanted to argue, but William Love, loosening the soil around the melon garden next to the corn, interrupted, shouting over the rail fence. "Nathaniel knows what he's talking about. Do as he says."

Grumbling, the silversmith left the corn garden and took his bucket past the new cottages and through the gate of the fort.

"Hello, Nat!" It was Ann Laydon, a basket on her arm half full of berries she had found in the brush at the edge of the clearing. The skin of her face and hands had grown red with the weather, and her belly was round beneath her skirts. She had a baby due in a few months. "Find any treasures under that corn?"

If no one had been within hearing distance, Nat would have scolded her severely. But he just sighed and looked back at his work. There was a little pleasure in knowing that it irritated Ann greatly to be ignored.

"Your skin has become as dark as a savage in this sun," said Ann. "Does that mean you want to be like them?"

Nat rubbed a mosquito bite on his chest and

chopped the soil around a corn plant with his spade, softening it and working out stones.

"Do you hear me, gardener?"

Nat pushed the loosened soil back around the plant.

Ann stomped her foot. "You are impolite indeed! Do you hear me?"

Nat walked to the next plant and began to chop.

"You'll certainly never be a rich man nor a gentleman with your foul manners!" said Ann. She blew a noisy puff of air through her lips and wandered away.

It was all Nat could do to keep from laughing out loud. However, he could hear a chuckle from William Love nearby.

And then William's chuckle stopped abruptly and the man said, "They have arrived!"

Another gardener in the corn replied, "God help us, they best have food. A lot of food."

Nat dropped his own spade and put his hand to his forehead, shading out the glare of the sun. There, nearing the settlement on the sluggish James River, were five ships. More men, and perhaps women and children as well. This place was going to be overrun. As the gardener had said, they best have food. And a lot of it.

There were shouts from the cottages around the fort and from within. Those who were well enough to be up and off their cots were rallying around to greet the new arrivals. The inhabitants of James Towne clustered side by side by the water, staring at the newcomers.

"Which ships are these, now?"

"I see men waving from the deck. They best be in good health, I tell you. We don't need any more folks who are ailing or dying."

"Pray God the Company has at last sent us men who can work. Farmers, carpenters, surgeons, and cooks."

"You think the Company knows how we fare in Virginia? If they sent us a farmer, I will give you my whole food ration for two days!"

Only the first ship, the largest one with a broken mast, was able to anchor close to the pier. The others dropped anchor behind it, and simultaneously, longboats were lowered. Bedraggled passengers climbed down the sides and into them with haste, like rats escaping a sinking vessel.

"Not surprising they are so eager to get off them stinking things," said William, standing near Nat. "I remember arriving. Land was the most blessed thing to me when the trip was done."

"Hmm," said Nat.

"Only thing," William continued, "they've no idea what they're getting into here. They shall be anxious to climb back up and squeeze down that 'tween deck once they see what we have waiting for them here. Is not the lush pastures and sparkling streams we were promised, to be certain!"

Several other men chuckled sourly. Nat crossed his arms across his bare chest.

John Smith, who had been standing near the rear of the gathering, strode forward onto the pier to be the first to speak. He'd taken time to straighten his hat and the ruff of his collar. The man never ceased to look dignified when the need arose.

Several pairs of hands in the first longboat rose in greeting as the little boat touched the pier. "Hello, there!" called a man in the front. "God be praised, we have found you! God be praised, we have found James Towne!"

"God be praised if there's ale aboard," said the recovering Edward Pising. "I'll drop to me knees in this mud and shout 'glory, hallelujah!' if we've good stout drink in them ships!"

Passengers in the longboat climbed onto the pier

and bowed wearily, gratefully, to John Smith.

"Think there be girls with the men, Nathaniel Peacock?" came a shrill voice. "That should please you, I would think." Ann was right next to him, standing at his shoulder. She wore a smirk on her face, and her hair was free around her shoulders, not pinned up properly.

"You only know what pleases yourself, Mistress Laydon," said Nat quietly. "Now go to your husband. And make a decent style with that hair of yours. It seems as if you fancy the ways of the Powhatan women, with it hanging down like that."

Ann's face drew up and her eyes flashed. She whipped about and stormed over to John Laydon, who put his hand on her shoulder but otherwise didn't seem to notice she was there. He continued to speak with the other men and nod in the direction of the ships on the river.

The other longboats docked at the pier and the passengers continued to unload. There were many men, and yes, a few women and several young children. With a surge of fear and anger, Nat noticed the sickness of more than half; they staggered, they coughed dark spittle onto the soil of James Towne. Some needed the aid of others to walk. Others were carried.

"What we needed was meat and bread," cried Edward Pising. "Not half-dead, worthless people."

Nat watched as the hoard walked, hobbled, and stumbled toward the gate of the palisade through the cluster of settlers. It was pitiful indeed, as Jehu Robinson would have said. Men clung to sick wives; children cried in their mothers' arms. One young woman in a soiled blue gown and shabby velvet cape wept silently as she walked to the fort.

As a man passed, Nat asked, "Why does that woman weep? She does not appear ill as do many others."

"Young Mistress Ford lost her husband on the journey over. He died of the sweating sickness and we dumped his body overboard. She is but eighteen years, had been married but a week before the ships left England, and is now a widow!" The man stroked his chin and cleared his throat. It was a rattly sound; this man was suffering with a lung problem himself. "But she is a stout one, she is. I've not seen her cry aloud nor tear her hair as some of the women have. Instead, she has shown nothing but kindness to others who suffered on the trip, giving them aid and comfort. What a disaster we have endured. Our flagship *Sea Venture* was blown off course and we fear they are lost."

"Dreadful," said Nat.

"Indeed," said the man. He then extended his hand. "My name is Peter Scott. And this is my wife, Martha." He motioned to the small-framed woman behind him, who nodded wearily at Nat. "God be praised, the three of us survived the ordeal on the sea."

Three? Nat wondered. But then he noticed that Mistress Scott was pregnant. How would baby Scott and baby Laydon endure James Towne?

Nat gazed again at the stoic woman in the dirty blue gown as she followed the shabby assembly into the fortress. Then he went back to his spade in the cornfield. There was nothing to do but wait for the order to build more cottages and bury those who would die before the next morning.

William Love also returned to his work in the patch next to Nat's. "Gabriel Archer and John Ratcliffe are back," he said. "I'm certain John Smith would have rather they'd been two of the dead, tossed to the sharks in the depths of the sea."

Nat didn't answer. He chopped for a while, as fast as he could to make the muscles of his arms sting so he wouldn't have to think. Shadows crawled across the ground and Nat chopped and smoothed and raked.

As he neared the corn plants close to the trees, something in the corner of his eye moved. Nat looked up.
There, peering from behind the needled branches of
a pine, was Laughing Boy. Nat's mouth dropped open.
He had not seen the Powhatan in nearly a year, and
the change was amazing. Laughing Boy was muscular
and very tall, no longer the thin child with whom Nat
had explored. His hair was no longer plain, but
adorned with shells and feathers. Perhaps he had
grown into a warrior. Laughing Boy smiled and gestured for Nat come into the woods.

Nat shook his head. There were too many men
around to chance leaving. But he pointed to the sun
and then lowered his flattened palm. *I will meet you
when the sun sets.*

Laughing Boy understood. He nodded, and then de-
parted.

"It will be good to see him again," Nat said to himself. "There is so much going on now with the new
settlers, no one will miss me if I sneak away after dark."

It was more difficult to leave at sunset than Nat had
thought it would be. Smith had ordered all able-bodied
men who were not posted as watch to either bury the
dead, nurse the sick, or get to work planting posts for
new houses. Even as it grew dark, he had men set many
fires ablaze so they could see and continue digging
holes and raising the skeletons of the huts. Soon moonlight added its glow and the work went on without
pause.

Nat had never gone alone into the forest at night
without a lantern. But if he were to take a light, he
would be spotted, and so, with only the aid of the
moon's glow, he left James Towne and carefully made
his way to the place he and Laughing Boy used to meet.
Crickets and tree frogs mocked him. Their tiny, dry

voices seemed to ask, "Why are you here? It's dangerous. Go back. Go back."

He picked up a thick stick and held it before him
like a club.

Laughing Boy was not in the usual meeting place.
Nat held the stick and sat on the ground after poking
with the stick to make sure he didn't sit on a snake.
He waited. And waited.

After what seemed like an hour, Nat brushed himself
off and prepared to return to James Towne. Maybe
Laughing Boy hadn't understood after all. Maybe he'd
decided he really didn't want to be friends with Nat.
He felt his way along between the trees with the stick,
straining to see in the waning moonlight.

The crickets picked up their chorus. "Go back, go
back, go back, go back."

And then another sound caught Nat's ear, and he
stopped short. It was the whistle of a bird. But it
seemed out of place in the night. Nat had only heard
that whistle during the day. His fingers tightened
around the stick. He could hear his heart pounding in
his ears.

"I'm just imagining the sound," Nat told himself after a moment of silence. "I've gotten jittery and my
mind is playing tricks. I am acting like a child." He
strode forward again, this time humming a simple tune
in his mind.

Then the bird's whistle came again, this time from
very close to his left.

And then there was one to his right, and one directly
behind him. There was a rustle of leaves.

Oh, God, I'm not imagining, Nat thought. *I'm being followed by—*

Hands grabbed him then, throwing him to the
ground, driving air from his lungs with a harsh grunt.
His eyes slammed shut with the agony.

"Help!" he managed. A hand jerked his helmet off. A knee punched into his chest, throwing bright sparks of pain through his whole body. His head was yanked back by the hair. A hank of it ripped out at the roots. There were wails around him, screams ghastly and loud and triumphant. Nat's arms were stretched out to the sides and pinned firmly to the ground.

He opened his eyes.

There, holding him like a helpless insect, were four Powhatan warriors. They were painted white and black, and their eyes twinkled in the dark. One had a club of stick and stone, and it was poised over Nat's head.

They are going to smash my skull!

They all laughed at Nat. The sound was as cold as the blade of a dagger.

Nat screamed, knowing at the moment that he did it was a mistake because he was showing cowardice and that was enough to make him worthy of death.

The warriors laughed again, a sound that pierced the air like a devil's cry. The one with the club raised it high, ready to bring it down.

God help me no I'm going to die!

And there was a flash of movement, and the club was knocked away. Nat gasped. He couldn't see anything but two forms wrestling against the backdrop of black trees. His arms were released as the other warriors joined in the struggle. And then someone dropped over Nat's body, protecting him.

One warrior shouted, and the one crouched over Nat snarled something back.

The warriors argued fiercely, but the one over Nat didn't move. For many long minutes, there were heated words in native tongue, between the standing warriors and the one who sheltered Nat. At last the four standing Powhatans could be heard leaving, walking off into the darkness and muttering to themselves.

The form pulled away from Nat. Nat rubbed his eyes with his fists and with effort, drew his legs under himself and sat. It was then he could see clearly, even though the moon offered little assistance. Laughing Boy had saved him. He had risked his own reputation, his own life, for Nat.

Laughing Boy shook his head and made a soft, regretful sound and offered his hand to help Nat to his feet. Nat found his voice. "Thank you," he whispered.

Laughing Boy, who Nat was certain knew no English, nodded and patted Nat on the shoulder. *You're welcome*, the gesture said. He understood the words of appreciation.

Laughing Boy helped Nat to the edge of the woods but would go no farther. Nat waved good-bye and limped back to the fort. When he got to his cottage, William had awakened and the lantern was lit.

"What happened to you?" William asked. "You've got gashes all over, and your eye is swelling shut."

Nat hesitated. He should say nothing, but he was so awed with what he had just experienced, he couldn't keep quiet. "I was rescued in the woods," he said. "I had gone for a midnight hunt and was attacked by four strong Powhatan warriors. They meant to bash in my brains, but another threw himself over me and would not let it happen."

William's eyes grew huge. "Indeed?" he said. "A savage saved your life?"

"Yes," said Nat. He lay down on his mattress and pulled his deerskin over his shivering legs.

The following day, word of the rescue had spread. Even John Smith came to Nat's cottage to speak to him about it.

"You were alone in the woods?" asked Smith, his arms crossed and his eyes narrow. "Who gave you permission?"

Nat answered, keeping his gaze downcast. "Forgive me, but with all the new arrivals and their dire conditions, I thought I might hunt a bit and bring in extra meat."

Smith said nothing, but stroked his chin. He stared out of the cottage window, then looked back at Nat. "I was rescued in such a manner, too. Pocahontas laid her head on mine to keep her father from killing me."

"That is amazing," said Nat.

"You don't believe me?"

"Oh, sir, of course! I only mean that God was surely watching you!"

"Of course He was," said Smith. "God likes me and has a special eye for me. How else could something like that happen?" He left the cottage.

He can't tolerate that I have such an amazing story! Nat wrote hastily on a page. *And now he makes my story his, and makes it more exciting that it is a princess and her father the Powhatan. Pompous! Self-important! And I hope the man never has chance to read my words.*

But neither Nat's tale nor Smith's mattered much. There was work to do among the sick and dying of James Towne. Remembering the rescue made Nat feel grateful, and amid all the sadness, it gave him a sense of wonder.

He wrote, *My friend saved my life. And he is no savage. His name is Laughing Man.*

28

September 2, 1609

John Smith was in the shallop with some of the soldiers when a powder keg exploded. It cut the man to pieces, burning him and tearing him at the same time. He is in his cottage, and although I've not peeked inside, they say it is all he can do to keep from screaming from the pain. He bites leather to keep his agony silent. There is talk he might die. Some say he should return to England if he is to live. What will happen here if he leaves? There is no one who can rule James Towne as well as Smith.

I think about Ratcliffe, Wingfield, and Percy. Did they plan this? Did they bribe one of the soldiers to light the keg in order to kill Smith? I will never know for certain.

Nicholas, Samuel, and I have been put on burial duty as well as gardening duty. There was a stocky and able boy who came with the August ship, one named Henry Spilman, but he was taken as a hostage to the natives just before Smith's accident, and so there are only three boys strong enough now for the digging of graves and removal of bodies. Over the past weeks, many of the new arrivals who were ill have died. I hate to touch the cold skin of the dead. I have to make myself think that they are indeed dead, no more than the carcasses of the deer and bear I have eaten. Mistress Ford must think me foul indeed, walking about with the stench of the dead on my hands. I wish that was not so, but I fear it is.

One of the dead early this morning was a little girl named Martha Angus. Her mother is also sick, but would not let go of the child when we went inside her cottage with our lanterns to remove the body. She just sat on the cot, crying, holding the child in a filthy blanket, kissing the crusted forehead and vomit-streaked lips. At last her husband took the child away and, as weak as he was, came with us to the newest place for bodies on the northwestern edge of the colony near the forest wall. The father made us promise that animals would not dig his poor child from the ground. I promised him, knowing it was a lie. At night it is all we can do to watch for natives, much less a determined fox.

There is little we can do. As I sit and write in the light of my lantern on this late night, I hear voices calling for Samuel and me. Another has died and we must take the body out.

Smith must recover. James Towne is failing.

❧ 29 ❧

October 3–30, 1609

JOHN SMITH WAS dying indeed. The dreadful wounds from the powder explosion had healed badly, and not even the surgeon knew how to put him right. Nat had at last found the courage to look in on the wounded leader, peering through the rear window of the cottage and heart sinking at the sight.

Smith was nearly a corpse, his face pale and scarred, his chest heaving with effort. The great cape hung, burned nearly to a rag, on the wall beside a cross. Reverend Hunt sat beside him, reading Scriptures aloud.

"He leadeth me in the paths of righteousness for his name's sake . . ."

Nat pulled away from the window and forced himself down to the fall garden to pull bugs from the pumpkins.

It was with much anxiety and sadness that the council president was put aboard a ship to go home. Prayers were offered up in the church that Smith return to England safely and that he recover quickly.

The citizens of James Towne watched the sail of

Smith's ship disappear down the river past the trees. Nat and Nicholas stood side by side, staring after the boat. Nat felt as though the sun was setting, not to rise again.

Look out for yourself, Nat, he thought. *Do you see what is happening? The colony is going to fall, likely to never rise again. Remember your own rule. Take care of yourself or you shall go down with it!*

John Ratcliffe, who stood closest to the edge of the river, turned to the gathering and said, "Do not fear, gentlemen and ladies. Godspeed to John Smith, but he is in God's hands now. I have plans which our fine Captain Smith would never have approved but which I have no doubt will lift us from this mire and bring prosperity, wealth, and comfort to us all."

There were murmurs, some of interest, some of doubt.

"Fear not, I am back in charge." With that, the man brushed through the crowd and strode back up the embankment and into the fort.

Nicholas shook his head, picked a piece of grass from the riverbank, and stuck it in his mouth to chew. "We're in trouble now if we weren't already," he said.

"We are for certain," said Nat.

In the weeks that followed, Ratcliffe did nothing to lift the colony from the mire. He spent his time with his gentlemen friends, mingling only with the other settlers at church services. With no supervision now, stealing among the citizenship became commonplace at night when guards were groggy and not very alert. The hogs and chickens, which Smith had ordered left unbutchered until spring, were snatched, one by one, and killed and eaten by those with enough energy to do so. It was a subtle but relentless feeding frenzy under the cloak of night.

And hunger was a great equalizer.

Nat stood in the doorway to his cottage long after Samuel and William had fallen into restless sleep. It was warm for an October night, and the breeze coursing through the fortress carried mixed scents of dead leaves, mud, and sickness. The stars overhead spattered the black sky like sparkling sand. From the cottages within the fort walls and those without came the sounds of coughing, groaning, crying, snoring. An owl cried from the forest.

Few men have been caught or put on trial for stealing from the animal pens and the storehouse, Nat thought. *At this moment, there are but five men inside the jail accused of taking grain, and these men were obviously clumsy! Why shouldn't I give it a try? I am perhaps the best-trained thief among us, and my stomach grumbles while there is food to be taken!*

"Yes," he whispered. "But when you have stolen in the past, it never robbed another of a chance to live."

But if I don't take it, someone else will, he thought. *Would I rather the food be taken by Wingfield or Ratcliffe, or perhaps the watch guard, or some other gentleman? It shall be taken regardless. It might as well be me.*

Nat snatched a small knife he had by his cot into the side of his shoe, stepped outside, and walked quietly around the cottage, past the empty pigpen to the chicken house, then held tightly against the wall and listened for any sign he'd been noticed. The helmeted guards on the bulwarks were not talking to one another, so Nat guessed they were too tired to chat or, God forbid, possibly dozing. The night watch had passed Nat's cottage just a minute earlier with musket, pistol, and lantern in hand, but he would not be around again for another few minutes. Nat knew that if there was a chicken left to be had, he would have it.

The door was latched, but there was a small window with reed-woven shutters tied closed. Nat cut the rope and pushed one side of the shutter open. The window was small, but Nat was thin now, and bony. He worked one arm through the window, then his head and shoulder, hearing with relief the soft chortle of a hen somewhere in the darkness. His second arm went through and with a bit of kicking, he fell headlong into the rotting straw of the chicken house.

Scrambling up, he put his head to the window to listen and look for the night watch. Again, nothing to see but darkened cottages and sheds, the massive, shadowed wall of the fort, and the silhouette of the guards on the bulwark.

There were several chickens in the house, ones John Smith had ordered left alone until spring with the other animals. Smith was right to make such an order. Taking these animals and the grain from the storehouse in the fall was just asking for dire circumstances come late winter and early spring.

But stomachs hurt now. And, as Nat had decided back at his cottage, if these birds didn't go to him, they would surely go to another thief.

He sat quietly until one of the five remaining chickens came pecking within arms' reach. Then he dove on it, snapping its neck with one swift and easy move. The other chickens, sensing danger, scrambled off. He cut off the head, threw it into the dark, and let some of the blood drain into his mouth. It was hot, salty, and thick, but not foul as he would have thought two years ago. The rest of the blood, he let drain into the straw. Then he began the job of stripping feathers. It was difficult, but he ripped as many off as he could, tossing them to the floor.

Stuffing the headless, nearly featherless bird into his shirt, Nat climbed back out through the window, tied the shutter back as best he could, looked carefully for the watch, then sneaked back to his own cottage, where

Samuel was thrashing in sleep and William was speaking in his dreams. Nat hid the chicken beneath his cot. When he was really feeling hungry, he would cook the bird and eat it. It was his now. Nobody could lay claim to it.

As he lay down for just a couple of hours sleep, pulling the mildewed blanket up to his chin, the cottage door slammed open. It was the night watch, waving his lantern.

"Peacock!" the man said sternly.

Christ have mercy! thought Nat. *I'm caught!*

"Sir?"

"And Collier! Up, the two of you. We've a dead man, Alexander Peavey, in a cottage outside. His brother alerted me. We need the body taken out."

"Oh, sir," said Nat. "Of course. Samuel, up, boy! We've work to do."

Nat put on his shoes, pretended to wipe sleep from his eyes, and went to the door. Behind him, Samuel fumbled for his own shoes.

The night watch raised the lantern and stared at Nat, frowning. "What is that? You've got blood on your face, boy!"

Nat touched his face. How careless he'd been! "I bit my tongue while sleeping, sir," he said humbly. "Dreaming the tongue was a slab of beef."

"And the blood on your shirt?"

Where I carried the chicken, Nat thought, and quickly said, "I bit my tongue quite hard, sir. It is paining me dreadfully, you can imagine."

"I can imagine indeed," said the night watch, looking at Nat, at his shirt, and at Nat's cot.

Then Samuel was there beside Nat, shivering in spite of the seasonable temperatures, saying, "Why do they have to die at night? Can't they wait a bloody few hours?"

The cottage was on the south side, outside the fortress, and it took a good two hours for the two of them to take the body out and bury it quietly near the forest. When Nat and Samuel returned to their own cottage, the sun was beginning to show to the east past the trees and down the river.

And the chicken Nat had stolen had been stolen.

❧ 30 ❧

November 1609

Most of the provisions were gone by the middle of autumn, and the citizens of James Towne began to wail to the councilmen to save them from starvation and destruction. This fall, the number of settlers was larger in spite of the deaths, and the fear of hunger seemed triplefold with the masses.

In early November John Ratcliffe declared loudly hat he would rescue the colony. He would take the shallop upriver and meet with the savages whom Smith had befriended and bring back plenty of grain and meat. Those who had the strength had gone down to the pier to send them off, and with as much pomp as he could muster, Ratcliffe herded forty-eight men into the shallop and they paddled west. Nat watched until the boat could no longer be seen beyond the bend.

"Will they have luck?"

Nat turned to see Mistress Ford behind him. She wore the same blue gown she had the day she had arrived in James Towne, but it was cleaner now. She smiled softly, a sadness at the corners of her mouth.

"Possibly," said Nat. He didn't want to lie to this woman. She seemed strong enough to take the truth. "But it can be very dangerous. The Powhatans have ideas different from ours. They do not believe we should be here, but at times they tolerate us. It is a mystery, and we are at its mercy."

The woman nodded. Then she said, "Do you have a moment? I need help."

Nat had meant to spend time skinning the few groundhogs that several men had brought to the fort the day before. The meat had been consumed already, but the skins, when cured properly, could be stitched together to make a blanket for the upcoming winter. But he said, "All right."

Mistress Ford led Nat to a cottage near a small sheep shed on the eastern side of the fortress. "This is my home," she said. "My name is Audrey Ford. I live here with Sally Martin and the couple Peter and Martha Scott."

I know, thought Nat. There wasn't a settler he didn't know by name now, or a cottage whose residents he couldn't name. But Mistress Ford, clearly a lady in spite of this land of despair, was still a lady, still gracious and polite.

He returned the official greeting. "I am Nathaniel Peacock. A pleasure." He bowed. It had been a long time since he'd bowed to anyone.

"Sally is dying," said Mistress Ford. "Of dysentery."

Nat stopped at the open doorway. Audrey went inside, then bid Nat come, too. He stepped into the shadows.

Sally was a specter beneath a fouled blanket. Her face had caved in on itself and most of her hair had fallen out. Her eyes were closed.

"I promised her she would see the sun once more before she died," said Audrey quietly. "I tried to lift her and take her out, but she is so limp I can't get hold of her to lift her. Will you help me, sir? It is her last wish. God will bless you, and so will Sally."

My job is the dead, not the near dead, Nat thought. *I have other things to do, damn it all.*

In a woven basket in the corner of the cottage were several dead, furry animals. Not groundhogs or squirrels, but rats, their tiny eyes glazed over, their skulls crushed. These people were already catching rats for food. Nat realized that it might not be long before rats would be considered good fare to all of the James Towne citizens.

Nat took a deep breath of the thick, putrid air. Then he went to Sally, slid his arms beneath her, and lifted her from the bed. She weighed nearly nothing. Her nightdress was wet with urine.

Audrey and Nat went outside, walking through wrinkle-nosed settlers and frightened children. They went to the riverside, Audrey holding Sally's bony hand. Nat stood on his favorite rock and turned Sally so the sunlight reflected from the river onto her face. The woman shivered, muttered something unintelligible, and sighed. Then, with a violent spasm, she died.

Audrey put her free hand to her face, burying her eyes for a moment. "Jesus had pity on her soul," she said. "Sally was a fine woman."

Audrey helped Nat dig Sally's grave near the graves of the many who had died since August. Audrey said a brief prayer, and thanked Nat for his assistance.

"Let me know if there is any other way I can help," Nat heard himself say. "I share a cottage with Samuel Collier and William Love, inside the fort by the pigpen. You can find me if you need me."

Giving a gracious but tired curtsy, Audrey walked back up to the cluster of cottages.

It wasn't long before Audrey sought Nat's help again.

The day after Sally died, Audrey found Nat and asked if he would show Peter Scott how to best dress a rat. Nat was patient with the fumbling young Peter, and the two of them had a laugh at the earnest attempt which left the rat in three pieces. In appreciation for Nat's time, Martha mended Nat's torn stockings. Then Nat helped Peter patch the roof on the cottage. In thanks, Audrey gave Nat her dead husband's shoes. She had saved them from the ship. Nat put them on and they fit well. He put his old, holey shoes in the corner of his cottage in case he might need them at another time.

In the midst of the confusion, frustration, and anguish of the colony, Nat had found a place of peace—in the home of the Scotts and Audrey Ford. The exchange of help was easy and Nat looked forward to each new request.

"You are a smart man," Audrey said one evening as they sat side by side on the stone by the river. She wore a yellow gown and her face, thin and drawn and pale, had been scrubbed clean. Her dark brown eyes stared off at the other side of the water. "You know how to build a home, to raise crops, to hunt and to fish. If we survive here in James Towne, you could easily become a councilor with your knowledge."

"Oh, I doubt that," said Nat. "I am not rich. I once thought I'd find gold and become a gentleman, but I don't know if that will ever happen. And only rich men are considered worthy of leadership."

"That is a silly idea," said Audrey. "My husband was not rich, but he was one of the wisest men I ever knew." She hesitated. "And so are you." Then Audrey reached into the deep pocket of her gown and brought out a small leather-bound book. "I want to give you this. It is a book of poems. Do you read?"

"Yes," said Nat. He took the book and before he realized what he was doing, he gave Audrey a hug. He thought she might slap him, but she only smiled more. "I write, too," said Nat. "I've got pages in my cottage. I've written my thoughts whenever I've had the chance to do so."

"May I read them someday?"

Nat nodded.

The next morning, Nat gave Audrey the loose pages to read. And the following evening, she gave them back. They had been sewn together into a true journal, with blank pages at the back. "Peter Scott gave me paper to give you more room to write," she said. "Keep on writing. Your words are precious. They are the words of a gentleman, Nat."

Nat blushed and stammered a thank-you. He slept with the journal under his arm that night. His dreams were pleasant.

On the morning of November 17, the shallop returned from the west. Nat, Peter Scott, and William Love, along with several other men, hurried down to the pier to unload the baskets of food that John Ratcliffe had promised to bring to the fort.

But there were no baskets of food. There were only sixteen men in the boat, and John Ratcliffe was not among them. Those in the boat nearly fell out, scrambling with their fingers and babbling madly.

"What happened?" asked William. "Where is the wheat and corn and venison? Where are Ratcliffe and the others?"

One soldier dropped facedown onto the grass and began to sob. "Dead," he said. "All dead. The Powhatans pretended to be civil, then when we disembarked, they captured up and took us to their village. And Ratcliffe, God pity him! Never have I seen such a terrible fate imposed on a man!"

Nat could taste bile in his mouth. "What?" he managed. "What did they do to him?"

None of the soldiers spoke for a long time. Then one said, "He was stripped naked and tied to a tree. The savages laughed and howled at him, and I knew it was going to be heinous. The women of the village came out then, and armed with sharpened mussel shells, scraped his flesh from his body and threw it into the fire for him to witness! They flayed his legs, then his stomach, stripping the meat away as if he were a deer tied to a stake. And Ratcliffe lived through this, screaming as if his soul were burning in the very pits of hell. When he died at last, he was nothing but bloody bones and twitching nerves."

"Christ have mercy!" cried Peter Scott.

"Christ did not have mercy on Ratcliffe," said one soldier.

"But we ran off," said another soldier. "And even through the rain of arrows, we few escaped. But we bring nothing back except our own miserable selves."

"God help us now," said William. "Smith is gone, the Powhatans are again seeking to destroy us, our leaders do not know how to lead, and we have little food as the last of it was consumed weeks ago. Our storehouses are bare, our cottages crumbling, and many of us sick. God help us."

"God help us," said the soldiers.

God please help us! thought Nat.

31

December 25, 1609

Christmas day. In London, Richard and I would celebrate by stealing a pig and cooking it on a fire by the Thames River. I dreamed of better days. I thought they would be here.

I don't even know how to dream of better days now.

There is madness in James Towne. Madness born of illness and death and starvation and dread. The only thing that keeps me from losing my mind are my three friends. Peter and Martha. And Audrey. She is kind, wise, and pretty. I suppose now I can't let her read my journal or she will see these thoughts and think me forward.

Audrey says I am a gentleman. What a strange thought. I am ragged and poor and dirty. Yet she sees a gentleman. I don't even know what it is to be a gentleman, or a man at that. Laughing Man stood up for me when he was in danger. He did what he believed right.

Perhaps that is what changes a boy into a man. Not years, not airs, not wealth. But bravery to say or do what is right.

What is right?

I wish I knew.

For I have witnessed a horror, one too difficult to imagine, but it was not my imagination, for my own two eyes told me it was real.

Many of the settlers stay inside their cottages now; few are able-bodied enough to go out in the biting cold to retrieve water for their household or cook the gruel we make from roots and bark and grubs. The soldiers who are well enough to keep watch at the bulwark do so, though their numbers have dwindled. About thirty men and women are strong enough to hunt for food, picking through the forest and dragging the rivers, but they come up with little. Several men have run off to live with the Powhatans in hopes they would survive better with the natives. Sometimes those of us at James Towne eat once a day. Sometimes we do not eat on a given day.

But I did not want to believe what I saw three nights ago.

Marcus Daniels, boy of fourteen, died just before sunset, and his parents helped Samuel and me remove the body to the burial site. The ground is dreadfully hard this time of year, but the four of us were able to make a grave not quite two feet deep. It was the best we could do, given the cold and given our strength. I went into the woods then, looking for an injured bird, an opossum, something slow-moving to kill to eat. There were a few shriveled berries on a crabapple tree, and their bitter taste was fine to my tongue. There were sluggish grubs, sleeping beneath the bark in a tree, and I tugged them free, crushed them with my teeth, and swallowed them down. But my hunger still clawed at my gut, insistent, determined.

It was on my return that I was aware of commotion in the burial ground. I paused at the edge of the woods, staring in the moonlight, and saw someone huddled over the fresh grave of young Marcus Daniels. His father, I suspected, or his mother, come to grieve in private while the rest of the settlement lay still in the cold embrace of a winter's night.

But then I heard the soft cough, and recognized it, and did not understand why he would be at the grave.

It was Nicholas Skot.

I walked closer, quietly, because I sensed he thought he was alone and to startle him might cause him to cry out and make the guard suspect we were natives on the attack, and shoot at us. But as I approached, moving along the brush and keeping to the trees, I knew I did not want to see what was before me.

But it was too late.

Nicholas had unearthed the body of Marcus Daniels, and had severed both hands and put them into a bucket. He was at work with his knife, cutting the forearm off at the elbow. He panted with effort. His breath was visible on the frosty air. I knew his intentions, and I gasped.

He heard me, and glanced up, his eyes as wide with fear as the eyes of a deer Laughing Boy and I once chased into the shallows of the river to slay. And then, in a whisper barely heard over the hushed whisper of the December breeze, he said, "It is nearly Christmas, Nat. Don't you understand? Christ was born for us, and He said, 'This is my body.' "

"Nicholas, you'll die for this," I said. "If anyone hears of it, they will execute you!"

"You won't tell," he said. I could hear the giddy insanity lacing his words. "My body, take and eat. I have to eat, Nat. I have to eat!"

With that, he scooped up his bucket and ran off into the darkness through the silent cottages and sheds.

I returned to my cottage, and said nothing.

What is right?

I cannot know.

There have been rumors the past two days that graves are being robbed and the dead eaten by our starving colonists. Our leaders say it is an abomination, but they cannot find out who is supposed to have committed this sin.

I will not say, for I do not know what is right.

I have always been proud that illness and hunger have never seen me worth their while. But I fear that is not the case now. I know now how it feels. If I had the strength, I'd journey deep into the woods and find Laughing Man. I would ask him for help. But I can't. It is all I can do to write this. And I am tired now. I must stop. I am so very, very tired.

❧ 32 ❧

January 8, 1610

"NAT, WAKE UP, please!"

Nat's eyes opened, then closed. He was so tired. He wanted to sleep another hour. Another year.

"Nat, wake up. I am sorry to come into your cottage without permission, but we need you. Martha is in very bad condition."

Nat opened his eyes again. Audrey stood over his mattress. He could not make out her face in the darkness, but her voice was laced with genuine fear. "Nat, I think Martha is dying. Please come!"

Nat sat up. His head reeled and he had to wait until it subsided. Then he forced his feet into his shoes and stood up. William and Samuel were still sleeping.

"Come," said Audrey. She threw Nat's cloak around his shoulders, grabbed his hand, and the two of them went outside into the bitter winter night. As they moved toward Audrey's cottage, the young woman said, "Peter has lost his wits with grief. If Martha dies, he will lose not only a wife but a child as well! He is talking out of his mind, Nat. He even tried to strike me away when I went to comfort him. I tried to put a hand on Martha's forehead and he shoved me back. What should we do?"

Nat tried to speak, but it was as if his lips were frozen together.

"At least hold Peter so I can tend Martha," said Audrey. "If I can nurse her beyond this bout of illness, I will, but I cannot if Peter will not even let me near her. Will you hold Peter?"

Nat managed to nod.

They stopped outside the door to Audrey's cottage. A strong gust of wind lifted her cloak and skirts, revealing white, stick-thin ankles in mud-coated shoes. "Peter, it is Audrey. I have Nathaniel with me. We are coming in to help."

There was a low growl, but nothing more. Audrey cast a desperate look at Nat, and opened the cottage door. They went inside. It was not much warmer inside than out.

A single lamp, sitting on the top of the Scotts' small trunk, burned with a dim, sputtering light. Nat's eyes had to adjust before he could even find Peter and Martha. And then he was able to make them out. Peter was crouched in the corner on the dirt floor, wearing only his long white linen shirt, holding Martha tightly in his arms.

"Peter, Nat is here. Martha needs our help. Please let me see her. Talk to Nat while I check on Martha to see what I can do for her."

Peter lifted his head. His eyes were as wild and dangerous as those of the mad dog Nat had killed in London. "Go away!" he snarled.

Martha and Nat took several steps closer. Peter tried to back farther into the corner. Martha groaned weakly, but her eyes did not open and she did not move.

"Peter, you are our friend," said Audrey. "Martha is our friend. We want to help."

Peter's teeth were bared. His lips twitched.

"Peter," said Nat. "Give Martha to Audrey. Come to the other side of the cottage with me. Let us talk."

There was a long moment of silence. Audrey said to Nat, "I gave him some acorn gruel, but he slapped it away. It was as though he no longer can even recognize food."

Nat nodded.

"Peter, listen to us," said Audrey.

Peter looked from Audrey to Nat to Martha in his arms. "Martha," he said. "My Martha."

"Peter," said Audrey.

Suddenly Peter jumped to his feet, wailing and tearing at the air. Martha rolled off his lap into a heap. Peter lunged at Audrey, grabbing her throat in his fingers. Audrey gasped and fell backward, dragging Peter with her. Nat's blurry mind cleared then; he threw himself at Peter. His arms wrapped about the man's waist and with all the energy Nat had, he wrenched Peter away from Audrey. Peter screamed and struggled. His ragged fingernails gouged into Nat's wrists and he bit Nat on the hand.

"Audrey, get out of the cottage. Go find more help. I can't do this alone!" cried Nat.

Audrey darted out of the cottage. Nat continued to hold tightly to Peter even though the man slashed viciously with his nails and chomped with his teeth. At last Nat got one leg beneath those of Peter Scott and knocked the man's body out from underneath him. Peter hit the floor with a cry and Nat held him down.

Nat leaned in close to Peter's face. "Listen to me, man! You are hungry, we all are! But you cannot let it consume you. You must be strong for yourself, for Martha and the baby. Help is coming. We will do all we can to see that Martha makes it through."

Peter's struggles grew weaker and weaker. *Pray God he is not dying, too*, Nat thought. But the man continued to breathe, irregular, shallow breaths. Then Peter looked at Nat. He said, "Nat? Please get off me. You are too heavy."

"You will not fight with me?"

"No," said Peter. "I will not."

Nat got up from the floor and gave Peter a hand to help him up, too.

"Martha," said Peter. "I must go to her."

"Yes," said Nat, "And we will do what we can to bring her back to health."

They went to the corner and Peter knelt by his wife. He lifted her head. And then he threw back his head and roared. "She's dead!"

Nat touched Martha's wrist. He put his finger beneath her nostrils and there was no air moving. Indeed, the woman had died.

"Peter," Nat began. "I am so very sorry, so—"

But Peter's mind snapped again in an instant. He drove his fist against Nat's chest, slamming Nat backward into the trunk. The lantern wobbled but did not fall. Peter ripped at his face and his clothes and babbled dreadful, insane nonsense.

Nat left the cottage. He found Audrey pounding on a nearby cottage door, and he took her hand to stop it.

"No one will help," said Audrey. "I've tried three homes and everyone says we are all sick and dying and they won't leave their own to help Peter and Martha."

"It doesn't matter now," said Nat. "Martha is dead. Peter is indeed distraught beyond reason, but I think it is best to leave him alone with her until he comes to his senses."

"Where shall I sleep, then?" asked Audrey.

Nat took Audrey to one of the empty barns and made her a pallet out of straw. Then he brought his one remaining deerskin to her, covered her, and bid her good night.

Back in his cottage, he recorded the events of the night. *Poor Peter Scott,* he wrote at the end of the entry, *Such a loss, both wife and baby. Perhaps he will find better luck in the passage of time. Perhaps things will turn for the better for all of us. How can it get any worse?*

33

MARTHA SCOTT'S BODY was found in Peter Scott's trunk, chopped into pieces and covered with salt. Her belly had been ripped open and the baby was missing.

Peter Scott was immediately put into the James Towne jail, a small building with no furniture, lanterns, nor fireplace. He was left there for several days, with only a handful of grain tossed in for his meals. The trial would come to pass quickly, as soon as the council could decide what to do about so horrendous a crime.

"He killed her," Nat heard one gentleman say as he collected firewood from the fort's community supply. "Killed her and ripped the child from her and tossed the baby into the river. Then he cut his wife up and salted her for food. He thought no one would look in that ghastly trunk!"

"Killed his own wife," said another man. "I am starving, but I would never murder! Satan has come to James Towne and lives in the person of Peter Scott."

Nat found his voice and said, "Peter did not kill her, she died."

But the gentleman scoffed. "You are his friend, you'd say anything. Now, hold your tongue before I accuse you of assisting in the murder, boy!"

George Percy took Peter Scott from the jail after several days and marched the young man to a tall tree just outside the palisade. As everyone gathered to watch, Peter was drawn up by his thumbs and hung there, his jaws clenched together, his eyes wincing with incredible pain.

"Getting what he deserves," said one man in the crowd.

"God save his soul," said one woman.

"Nat, I was not there when Martha died," Audrey said, tears of frustration and pity coursing down her face. "You were there. Tell them what you saw."

But Nat shook his head. He might be accused of killing Martha, too. *Peter, I'm sorry! There is nothing I can do!*

Percy proceeded to question the tortured man hanging from the tree. "Peter Scott, did you murder your wife, Martha, and cut her into pieces?"

Peter did not move. Nat could see tears on the man's cheeks, but there was no sound.

"Did you cut her into pieces and throw your infant into the river?"

Peter did not answer. Cloth bags were tied to Peter's ankles and filled with stones to weigh Peter and make the pain even more terrible. The questioning went on for fifteen minutes. Nat stared at the ground. He could no longer endure the expression on Peter's face nor the agony in Audrey's eyes.

And then there was a cry of triumph from George Percy, and Peter Scott was cut down from the tree. "He admitted his offense," Percy told the crowd. "He nodded at the last question. His nod confirmed our accusations. This man is a murderer and shall die!"

Nat looked up at last. Audrey said, "Peter did not nod. His head spasmed and Percy, looking for anything to end this ordeal, said he saw a nod! What shall we do? Peter was mad with hunger, and so his tormented mind reasoned that Martha would be food after she died. But he did not kill her! We must stop the execution of Peter Scott!"

Nat turned away from Audrey. There was nothing he could say.

Peter Scott was returned to the jail and a pyre was built in the center of the barren cornfield. All men who were able piled brush and sticks and branches together and planted a post in the center. Nat feigned illness to keep from participating. He lay on his mattress and tossed with anxiety and rage. At Peter for losing his mind and butchering his dead wife's body. At Martha for dying. At Audrey for being kind and drawing him into association with the Scotts. At George Percy for believing torture could secure truth. And at himself for having no courage to say what needed to be said.

The next morning, in the bitter cold, all those who were not sick in bed turned out for the punishment of Peter Scott. George Percy brought the torch, and made an impassioned speech, gesturing with the torch at both the condemned and at the witnesses. His words were punctuated with puffs of mist. He stomped his feet to keep warm, but on and on he rambled about God and the devil and Peter Scott's obscene acts.

Peter, his feet without shoes, and wearing only a torn shirt and moth-eaten trousers, had been lashed to the center post. He stared up at the sky. Every few moments he would shudder with the cold.

"We are Englishmen," said Percy to the settlers. "We are civilized, and will not tolerate less. Hanging is not good enough, not strong enough, for such a deed as Peter Scott performed. He must suffer and we will see that he does."

There were murmurs from the group, some in agreement, some laced with sadness for what Peter was about to endure.

"Peter, have you anything to say before you are sent out of this life?"

Peter said nothing. But then his head turned, and he looked directly at Nat.

Nat felt the stare as surely as a knife to his heart. He put his hand inside his cloak and drew out that which he had brought to the execution, that which he didn't really believe he'd have the courage to show.

"George Percy, sir!" shouted Nat. Audrey turned and stared at Nat with wonder. The mumbling in the crowd quieted. "Percy! Listen to me now, if never before. I must tell you something, and you must hear me out. I know for a fact that Peter Scott did not kill his wife."

"Don't listen to him, Percy!" shouted a gentleman. "He is Scott's friend."

"Let him speak," said Percy.

Nat held up his journal. It was curled and soiled, but inside was a record of the night of Martha's death, the details of what had happened. Nat said, "Most of you here know me. And those of you who do know I don't have friends. I have avoided friends ever since I came to James Towne. I have preferred to be alone, to take care of myself. But what I say is truth, God as my witness."

"Continue," said Percy.

"I went to the home of Martha and Peter the night she died. Audrey Ford called me and I came, hoping to calm the man as Audrey nursed the poor woman. I was with Peter and Martha when she took her last breath. I wrote of it in my journal, and I offer it now as testimony to the facts."

Percy held up his hand. "Mistress Ford, is Peacock giving us an honest statement?"

Audrey said, "I did indeed call him. Peter was crazed with heartache for the dire condition of his wife. I was not there when she died, but I can say Nathaniel Peacock would tell the truth."

There was mumbling in the crowd. Then Nat continued, "Please, sir, read my journal aloud and let Peter be charged with only the cutting of his wife. Surely that is not an offense requiring death."

George Percy squinted at Nat, then Peter, then the journal. "Bring that record to me, boy," he said.

The crowd parted as Nat worked his way to Percy. Some looked at him as he passed as though they hoped the journal might stop the burning. Others scowled as if they were afraid it would.

"Here, sir," said Nat. He gave the booklet to Percy. Percy handed the torch to the torch man. Nat took a deep breath. He couldn't imagine what trouble he'd be in for rescuing Peter, but right now it didn't matter. He had no choice.

I have no choice. Richard, this is for you, too.

Percy flipped through the pages, then tossed the journal onto the pyre. "Make-believe," he declared to the settlers. "Anything to try and rescue this demon!"

"Accuse Peacock of conspiring to murder Martha Scott!" came a cry.

Percy paused, then shook his head and said, "There is no indication that Peter acted in any way but alone. Peacock is just trying to stall what must happen. Now we shall have justice. Peter Scott will face our fire here in this life and hellfire in the next."

Percy nodded to the torch man, who lowered the flame to the kindling and waited until it began to smolder and smoke. The journal caught the first licks of flame and went up like dry leaves.

Nat watched, dumbfounded, horrified. Audrey came over, took his arm, and buried her face in his sleeve. She couldn't watch as the fire grew stronger and stronger, working its way to the center pole where Peter Scott stood, his eyes closed.

Women in the gathering broke into sobs. Men mumbled uncomfortably. Nat said nothing. He stared into Peter's face, and thought, *Peter, I pray it goes quickly for you.*

The fire reached Peter's legs and caught the fabric of his trousers instantly. The blaze raced up his chest to his face. There were several seconds of silent twitching and shaking. The smell of roasting flesh was sharp and pungent. And then, with an unbearably long scream of supreme anguish, Peter Scott gave his consciousness and life to God.

Only a few remained to watch the man reduced to cinders. Nat led Audrey back to her cottage. She sat without a word on her cot, and Nat sat next to her, holding her gently. He could feel her quiet weeping as his chest grew warm and wet.

"You did a good thing," came a voice from the door. Nat looked over to see William Love. "Someone had to speak up for Peter. I can't believe he killed his wife, either. Thank you for trying."

Nat nodded and William withdrew. Minutes later, Edward Pising looked into the cottage. "Master Peacock? You were brave to speak out at such a moment. I didn't know Peter Scott well, but I know in my soul that he could not have killed his wife. He was a fine man. He should not have died. But you gave his death some dignity."

"Thank you," said Nat.

A handful of other men and women stopped by to

tell Nat of their appreciation for his courage. Nat thanked them all in turn.

Night came. Audrey fell asleep, curled up on her cot, and Nat gazed at her for a moment, and then covered her gently with the deerskin. He touched her hair and bid her a sleep without dreams.

He went back to his cottage and found that Samuel Collier had put three sheets of paper on his mattress as well as a pen and small well of berry ink.

🦋 34 🦋

January 16, 1610

    The winter rages on. We've seen snow and sleet and more of us dead. The frozen ground is hard to dig for graves, and our arms can barely wield a shovel. We had nearly five hundred when John Smith was sent back to England. Now there are barely one hundred. Should we have come? I do not know. Will we become like the colony of Roanoke Island and vanish without a trace? I do not know that either. We are in the hands of time and fate.

    But I think I have become a man. I have found friendship is a good thing, and that it is better to work together than apart. Lessons which may serve me well if I live. I hope I will.

    Audrey is meeting me in a few minutes. We are going to collect acorns. There might still be a few in the forest which can be cooked, and perhaps if I have the strength, I can climb a tree like Laughing Boy taught me and watch for a lumbering groundhog.

    Together. It is a good word. Whether for another week or a lifetime. God get us all through this.

    Together.

Available by mail from

TOR
FORGE

1812 • David Nevin
The War of 1812 would either make America a global power sweeping to the pacific or break it into small pieces bound to mighty England. Only the courage of James Madison, Andrew Jackson, and their wives could determine the nation's fate.

PRIDE OF LIONS • Morgan Llywelyn
Pride of Lions, the sequel to the immensely popular *Lion of Ireland,* is a stunningly realistic novel of the dreams and bloodshed, passion and treachery, of eleventh-century Ireland and its lusty people.

WALTZING IN RAGTIME • Eileen Charbonneau
The daughter of a lumber baron is struggling to make it as a journalist in turn-of-the-century San Francisco when she meets ranger Matthew Hart, whose passion for nature challenges her deepest held beliefs.

BUFFALO SOLDIERS • Tom Willard
Former slaves had proven they could fight valiantly for their freedom, but in the West they were to fight for the freedom and security of the white settlers who often despised them.

THIN MOON AND COLD MIST • Kathleen O'Neal Gear
Robin Heatherton, a spy for the Confederacy, flees with her son to the Colorado Territory, hoping to escape from Union Army Major Corley, obsessed with her ever since her espionage work led to the death of his brother.

SEMINOLE SONG • Vella Munn
"As the U.S. Army surrounds their reservation in the Florida Everglades, a Seminole warrior chief clings to the slave girl who once saved his life after fleeing from her master, a wife-murderer who is out for blood." —*Hot Picks*

THE OVERLAND TRAIL • Wendi Lee
Based on the authentic diaries of the women who crossed the country in the late 1840s. America, a widowed pioneer, and Dancing Feather, a young Paiute, set out to recover America's kidnapped infant daughter—and to forge a bridge between their two worlds.
